THE

DANCING MAHARANI

and Other Stories

Happy birthday!

♡

THE
DANCING
MAHARANI

and Other Stories

Ranjit Kaur

For my mum Harbhajan Kaur,
my sisters Parmjit and Abnash,
my dearest Paulette,
and for everyone who has experienced migration.

CONTENTS

Good Buys

I

Harpreet's mother was unwell. Her father had written to her in his neat Urdu script on the blue tissue-like aerogramme. These arrived fortnightly, bearing an Indian stamp, bringing all the news from back home. It was nothing serious or anything for her to worry about, he wrote. But Harpreet suspected he was lying. Otherwise why mention it at all?

Harpreet re-read the letter several times. Over the next few days she worried. Finally, her mind was made up. She would visit her mother in India and spend time helping her recover.

It was 1979 and air fares to India were not cheap, but Harpreet knew that Mr Khan who ran the travel agency in Leith would get her a good deal. She would take her daughters, Ritu and Meena, with her. It would be good for them to see their grandparents and other relatives again. She felt it essential that they maintain a link to their Indian heritage. This was something the girls' father had also felt strongly about.

After her husband had dropped dead one fine June day when the girls were still small, Harpreet had managed to save some money from doing two jobs. She worked part-time at the hospital as a cleaner, and also sewed clothes at home for a factory. Her elder daughter, Ritu, was now working and contributing to the household running costs. Meena was in her final year at school. Harpreet decided they would go to India in July after Meena's final exams. A six-week holiday would do them all good.

Harpreet went to see Mr Khan, who ran his travel agency and money exchange from a little run-down shop in a back street in Leith. Mr Khan was a polite and cheerful man, originally from the Punjab in Pakistan.

"Good afternoon, sister!" He stood up to greet Harpreet enthusiastically when he spotted her walking into his shop. Smiling broadly, he signalled for her to sit down.

"I haven't seen you for a while," he said. "All is well with your family?"

"All fine, thank you," replied Harpreet, seating herself.

"Can I get you some tea, coffee maybe, or a cold drink?" Mr Khan asked whilst lowering himself into a big leather swivel chair.

"No thank you."

"No problem. *Kheyiji*, please tell me how I can assist you today?" He leaned back into the padded backrest.

Harpreet leaned forward. "I need three tickets to India. Preferably landing in Amritsar rather than Delhi. What have you got on offer?"

Mr Khan spread his hands on the desk.

"I can get you a very good deal, sister. Tickets direct from London to Amritsar. At a very reasonable price."

"Who with?" Harpreet asked. "Air India? Gulf Air? Thai Airways maybe?"

"None of these," Mr Khan replied. "At present, there is only one airline that flies to Amritsar for such a good price."

"Is it Russian?" Harpreet asked nervously.

"No. It's Afghani Airways."

Harpreet took a few seconds to register this information.

"But I've never heard of them."

"Sister, they are the best. *Pukka desi*. Like our own. Delicious food, comfortable flights. And best prices. Eight hundred pounds for three return tickets. Good, no?"

Harpreet was impressed. Last time she flew with Air India it cost considerably more than that.

"Sounds very good," she said. "Do our people use them a lot?"

"All of the Punjabis in Leith and beyond," replied Mr Khan with a smile.

"Well, here are my dates and the passenger details," said Harpreet, pulling a piece of paper from her handbag.

"Leave it with me. I will call you in a few days when I have it all arranged," said Mr Khan, taking the piece of paper from her.

"When do you need the money?"

"Sister, don't worry about that. You can pay me when you come to collect the tickets."

Harpreet nodded gratefully. That arrangement suited her fine.

II

"So Mum, where does this flight stop?" asked Ritu whilst fastening her seatbelt.

"I don't know," replied Harpreet, "but wherever it does, we will be able to have a look around."

Her nephew, Anmol, had driven them to London, stopping for a night at Harpreet's cousin's house in Coventry. It was a long drive, and it was nice to break the journey to see family, even though it did mean that their three heavy suitcases were now even heavier. When cousin Balbir had asked them to take some shirts for his father and cardigans for his mother Harpreet felt unable to refuse. Amidst much giggling, Ritu and Meena had to sit on the suitcases to close them because they were so full.

Once Ritu had settled down in her seat, she looked across to her sister. Meena had stuffed half the contents of her handbag into the pocket of the seat in front, and was flicking through an Indian film magazine that Balbir's wife had given her.

Ritu appraised her co-passengers. They appeared mostly Indian. It was a packed flight.

As the plane took off, she looked through the window. She spotted a fly trapped between the inner and outer windows and wondered how it got there.

An hour or so later, the attendants began serving some unappetising smelling fare consisting of rice and inedible curried vegetables. The rice had a strong, bitter flavour which Ritu tried to identify but failed. She concluded it might just have been over-cooked.

Both Ritu and Meena dozed for a while whilst Harpreet read a magazine. They woke to an announcement from the captain that the flight would soon be arriving at its first destination, Istanbul. There would be a stopover of an hour and passengers were asked to leave the plane to allow cleaning to be done.

While the plane was taxiing to its stand, the stewardess announced that the terminal building was still under construction and for this reason there was no speaker system for announcements. Passengers were advised to stay in the seating area and not wander off.

Harpreet, Ritu and Meena gathered up their belongings and joined the other passengers queuing to exit the plane and board the bus which would take them the short distance to the terminal. Night was falling and the airport was lit up brightly. They made their way into the building. Meena ran forward and found three seats together, signalling for the others to join her. The room smelled of fresh paint and concrete. Cables dangled from the ceiling and the walls had not yet been plastered. The trio sat looking around them. The room was devoid of shops or cafes. Gradually, as the passengers relaxed, the sound of chatting echoed around the room.

Meena spotted a foot-wide gap in the wall behind her seat. She got up and walked over to look through it. What she saw made her very excited. She quickly returned to the others.

"Mum! There's a guy selling jewellery on the other side," she said, pointing to the gap.

Harpreet looked interested.

"Really? What is it? A shop?"

"No, he's got a cart thing, but he's got loads of jewellery on it. Shall we take a look?"

Ritu looked at her mother and sister in alarm.

"No! We can't. We were told to stay here. There are no announcements, remember?"

Harpreet stood up. She and Meena could not resist jewellery.

"Don't worry," she reassured Ritu, "we will see people leaving if our flight is called."

"No Mum, I don't think we should."

Harpreet and Meena ignored Ritu as they squeezed themselves through the gap. Ritu felt anxious, but followed them anyway. The other passengers didn't seem to notice their disappearance.

The man with the jewellery cart looked with surprise at the three women emerging through the gap. His lined face broke into a wide smile when he realised they were customers.

"Hello!" he said, beckoning with both hands whilst adding something in Turkish. When it became apparent they didn't understand, he spoke to them in heavily accented English. "Come and see my beautiful rings, necklaces and earrings."

Harpreet and Meena needed no encouragement. They began examining the brightly coloured jewellery. Ritu looked nervously around her.

"Please try," the man encouraged. Ritu thought he looked tired.

They put the rings on their fingers and selected a few bracelets.

"Here, Ritu," said Harpreet, "this lovely green stone ring will look good on you."

Ritu tried on the ring. She had to admit, it did look nice. Spotting an opportunity, the man took out a tray-load of rings from under the cart.

"More here. Please look!" he said.

They admired the rings as they made their selection. The minutes ticked by until they were finally ready to pay for their purchases. Harpreet pulled out her purse and asked the man what currency he would accept.

"I take Turkish lira, sister, or even British pound – both are good," he said. He suddenly swept all the jewellery off the counter in a single rapid movement into a paper bag. "You pay me now!" he said urgently. "Quickly!"

Sensing trouble, Ritu turned to look behind her, and to her alarm saw two soldiers bearing guns walking towards them.

A heated exchange ensued between the soldiers and the cart owner. He pointed accusingly at the trio of women, indicating that they spoke English.

"What are you doing here?" one of the soldiers barked.

Ritu opened her mouth to try to explain, but the soldiers began talking fast and loud in Turkish to the jewellery man.

"He says it's not his fault. You came through the wall," said one of the soldiers.

Ritu looked across at the shocked faces of her mother and younger sister.

"We are from the Afghani Airways flight. We saw the cart through the gap in the wall. Sorry to cause a problem, but it's okay, we will go back," said Ritu.

"Back where?" the first soldier yelled pointing at the gap in the wall.

Harpreet, Ritu and Meena peered through the gap. To their horror, the room was empty.

"The flight is ready to leave," said the other soldier.

"We are very sorry," Meena mumbled, fluttering her eyelashes at the soldiers and biting her lower lip.

The soldiers looked at each other. Then one of them spoke quickly into his walkie-talkie.

"Follow us. Quick!"

Ritu glanced at the jewellery man. He banged his fist on the counter and said something in Turkish that sounded rude. Then they all turned and ran down the corridor after the soldiers, leaving the man still cursing.

After a few minutes they reached a door marked "Exit". Harpreet had a stitch and clutched her side, puffing loudly.

One of the soldiers opened it. "Outside," he shouted.

They all ran out and were met by another soldier in a jeep, who gestured to get in.

Now that she realised they were not going to miss the plane, Ritu smiled at all the drama and shouting – she felt like she was in an action movie. The three of them clung to the side bar as the soldier drove like a maniac across the tarmac to the waiting aeroplane. Harpreet looked green, but Ritu and Meena struggled to hold back their laughter.

A stewardess peered out of the doorway of the plane.

The girls got out of the jeep and dashed up the ramp-stairs, while Harpreet puffed her way up more slowly.

"Sorry, sorry," they muttered as they passed through the doorway.

The frosty reception the stewardess gave them was nothing compared to the dagger looks they received from their co-passengers who tutted and muttered as they made their way to their seats.

They were still belting themselves in when the captain's voice came over the speaker.

"Good news, everyone! We've located our three missing passengers and I'm pleased to say we have a new slot in ten minutes. Apologies for the delay but we will be taxiing for takeoff soon."

Ritu and Meena were mortified and sank deeper into their seats. However Harpreet didn't seem bothered. She turned to Ritu and said, "Now what is he saying? Are we going soon?"

Ritu glared at her. "Shush, Mum. Yes, we are going soon."

Harpreet opened her Urdu magazine and without a hint of irony asked, "So what's keeping him here now?"

III

Ritu looked out of the window of the aircraft. It was early morning and the land below was sandy coloured and hilly. It looked quite barren, and she could not see any sign of life.

The captain announced that they were approaching Kabul where the flight terminated. Ritu and Meena exchanged shocked looks. They were meant to be travelling to Amritsar! They listened intently to what he was saying. Passengers travelling onwards to Delhi should wait in the transit lounge, he said, and ground staff would direct them where to go. Passengers travelling to Amritsar, however, should clear customs and immigration, following which they would be taken by bus to a hotel in Kabul. Judging from the noisy reception this announcement received, it was clear that this was news to the passengers travelling to Amritsar.

Ritu and Meena turned to Harpreet.

"Mum, did you know we had to stay a night in Kabul?" asked Meena.

From the startled expression on their mother's

face, they had their answer.

"Mr Khan didn't mention it," she said.

"Can I look at the tickets, Mum?" Ritu asked.

Harpreet retrieved her handbag from under the seat in front of her. She took out the tickets and handed them to Ritu who studied them carefully.

"They have our arrival in Amritsar tomorrow morning, Mum. Is this the date you gave Nanaji?"

"Yes," Harpreet replied, "I just assumed the time difference accounted for that."

"So at least Nanaji will be at the airport tomorrow to meet us."

"A day in Kabul might be interesting. Anyway, they will ensure we have accommodation and we can have a look round." Harpreet gave Meena a reassuring look and patted her knee.

Ritu was not convinced of her mother's attempt to make this sound like a great adventure. But then she saw the anxious expression on Meena's face and realised what her mother was doing.

"It'll be fine," she said.

The captain skilfully manoeuvred the plane between the mountaintops and they landed with a bump on the runway. Dust rose around them and for a few minutes it was difficult seeing anything. Even before the plane came to a standstill, there was a sudden eruption of frantic activity as passengers stood up and tried to get their bags down from the overhead compartments.

Ritu could never understand why people behaved like this. The stewards tried to make people sit down but eventually gave up. Bags tumbled out of overhead lockers and passengers tripped over each other as they pushed to get towards the exit.

Ritu stared out of the window to distract herself from the commotion. A lorry arrived with the stairs in tow and slowly began aligning itself with the front exit door. She noticed that a truckload of armed soldiers had pulled up next to the plane.

"Nice welcome," she thought, wishing they too were flying on to Delhi.

Watched closely by the soldiers, the passengers disembarked and boarded the bus, which took them to the terminal building. Ritu noticed that photographs of a grey-haired, serious looking middle-aged man, with a neat moustache and piercing eyes, seemed to be everywhere. She wondered who he was. He looked like a professor.

They were marched through the terminal building and told to have their passports ready for inspection.

Somehow, Harpreet, Ritu and Meena found themselves near the front of the queue. The immigration officer was a tall, well-built man with a thick bushy moustache which matched his eyebrows. He wore a bright white half-sleeved shirt and black trousers, and stood behind a table. Unsmiling, he spat out instructions at the nervous couple in front of him.

"Passport! Open your bags."

He peered into a bag and pointed at the bottles inside.

"What's this?" he bellowed.

The poor man who owned the bag looked embarrassed.

"Whisky, sir. Gifts for my family back home."

"One bottle only allowed," the immigration officer snarled. "Take them out and put them on the table."

The passenger took out two bottles and placed them on the table.

"But, sir," he stammered, "one bottle each isn't it? One is mine and one is my wife's. She is here." He pointed to the demure, *sari*-clad woman standing beside him.

The immigration officer's eyebrows twitched.

"Yours?" he said accusingly.

She nodded, keeping her eyes downcast.

He took their passports from them.

"You will get these back tomorrow. Welcome to Afghanistan. Now move on."

Harpreet, Ritu and Meena were next. Harpreet handed over their passports. The officer flicked them open and looked carefully at each photograph. He raised his head and looked at Ritu.

"What is that?" he said pointing to the camera around her neck.

"It's a camera," she replied, her heart thumping.

"I have never seen a camera like it. Are you sure it's a camera?"

"Yes, it's a Polaroid camera. It takes photos and produces them instantly."

She wished she hadn't brought the camera with her. She thought it would be a novelty in India, especially for her relatives who seemed constantly surprised by western technology. But now it was going to be her downfall.

The immigration officer stroked his moustache.

"Imran!" he bellowed. "Come here!"

Ritu tensed as the whole queue of passengers behind her leaned forward for a better view.

Imran turned out to be a soldier with an automatic gun.

Ritu felt sick. Having avoided being shot in Istanbul, she thought, she was going to be killed at Kabul International Airport instead.

Harpreet looked as if she was about to pass out.

Meena, however, was pushing forward for a clearer look.

"Please," said the immigration officer, his face breaking into a wide smile, "you take photo of me and my brother-in-law, Imran?"

Ritu nearly fainted with relief.

"Of course," she said, "but the film is in the bag and I need to load it and fix the flash."

"No problem. Please go ahead," said the immigration officer, beaming.

Ritu opened her bag, her hands shaking. She took out the film and flash-cube.

Meena whispered in her ear, "You do realise that we are all dead if the photo doesn't turn out?"

"Thanks for the reassurance," Ritu replied.

Harpreet looked nervously at her elder daughter.

"You have used it before, Ritu?" she asked.

"No Mum, the film is very expensive. I was hoping not to do this until we got to India."

"*Waheguru, waheguru*," said Harpreet, praying under her breath.

The immigration officer was in no hurry. He chatted to Imran as they flattened their thick, black hair and tweaked their moustaches to make them curl fiendishly at the ends.

"Ready. Say cheese!" said Ritu.

The immigration officer put his arm around Imran's shoulder and they grinned as the flash exploded.

Ritu took out the photo and waved it slowly to allow it to dry.

Imran and the immigration officer looked on in anticipation.

Slowly the picture began to emerge. To Ritu's relief, it was a good, clear picture. She waited until it was completely dry and she handed it to the immigration officer.

He grinned like a Cheshire cat as he shared it with Imran and a few of his other colleagues who had gathered around to see what was going on. Eventually he looked up at Ritu.

"Please may I keep the photo to show my wife?"

"Of course," she replied.

"Many thanks. My name is Khaled." He stretched out his hand and Ritu shook it.

"My pleasure. I am Ritu and this is my mother, and my sister, Meena."

Khaled shook their hands too.

"I have to keep your passports until you return tomorrow for your flight," he said. "Welcome to Afghanistan! Please now follow Imran. He will escort you to the bus."

Imran smiled as he led them through the arrivals hall to the waiting bus. He said something to the driver before they boarded.

Khaled had been so pleased with the photo that he took everybody else's passport quickly and waved them through. Not another question was asked or bag searched. The other passengers were so grateful they thanked Ritu effusively when they got on the bus. It was as though the incident in Istanbul had never occurred.

The bus was ready to leave. The driver signalled to Imran who got on and approached Ritu's seat.

"I have told the driver that you are Khaled's guests. He will ensure that you are looked after at the hotel. Please let the hotel manager know if you need anything."

Ritu thanked him. He bowed his head and put his hands together before departing. Ritu felt like she was a celebrity. She noticed that he stood waiting and watching until the bus departed.

IV

The road from the airport seemed empty at first, but as they reached the outskirts of Kabul, it began bustling with people transporting goods piled high on wooden carts. The men had dark coloured turbans on their heads and wore loose-fitting *salwars* and *kameezes*. Women were covered from head to foot in sky blue burkhas. Ritu had only ever seen pictures of women in burkhas and she was fascinated, wondering what the women underneath looked like. As the bus moved through more affluent areas, she noticed younger men and women in jeans, T-shirts and skirts.

There were also large billboards featuring the grey-haired man whose photo she had noticed at the airport.

The hotel was basic but clean. Khaled obviously had some influence, because when they arrived the bus driver said something to the man at the check-in desk. Whatever it was ensured that they were given a large en suite room and told that they had only to phone reception and Karim would be of service.

Karim was summoned and introduced to them. He was a gawky young man with blue eyes that shone out from his brown tanned face. His auburn coloured, shoulder-length hair was tucked behind his ears. He had a toothy grin and wore well ironed jeans and a *kurta* that reached down almost to his knees.

He looked pleased to see them, especially Meena who received a bigger smile and an approving glance.

"I take your bags to your room for you, yes?" Without waiting for an answer, he lifted the heavy suitcases on to a trolley and led the way to the lift.

When they got to the room, he insisted on showing them around.

"If you need anything, please phone and ask for Karim," he said. "I will come immediately."

Harpreet pressed some Afghani notes into his hand. She had exchanged some money downstairs at the reception desk.

"Thank you, Karim," she replied. "Please could we get some tea?"

"Most certainly! I bring now," and he scuttled off.

There were two double beds in the room, each covered with a colourful Afghani blanket. Harpreet took off her sandals and laid claim to the bed by the window, while Meena and Ritu lay on the other.

"Blimey!" Meena exclaimed. "What a journey! My sister, the star photographer!" She poked her sister in the ribs.

"Still one more day to go," said Ritu, poking her back.

The receptionist had told them that the bus would take them back to the airport at half past five the next morning.

"What shall we do now?" Meena asked.

"Let's go to the bazaar," suggested Harpreet. "We could ask Karim to come with us and we might find some more jewellery."

Meena got up from the bed.

"Great idea, Mum. When can we go?"

Ritu was not keen on shopping. However, the drive from the airport had been interesting and she was keen to see more of the city.

Just then there was a knock at the door. Karim entered, carrying a tray with cups of tea and biscuits. He placed them on the table.

"Thank you, Karim," said Harpreet. "We are thinking of visiting a bazaar. Would you be able to take us?"

"Of course," Karim nodded with a radiant smile. "You want to go now?"

Harpreet thought for a minute.

"No, give us time to relax and freshen up. Can you come back in an hour?"

"Most certainly," replied Karim. He glanced at Meena.

Exactly an hour later, Karim, without knocking, opened the door.

Harpreet was not impressed. "Karim!" she shouted. "Please knock first. We may not have been decent."

Karim looked sheepish.

"Sorry, madam. I forgot as I am too excited about taking you all to the bazaar."

They looked at each other, puzzled.

When they left the hotel they realised why Karim was so excited. Everywhere they went, people gathered around them, gesturing, pointing and chatting loudly in a local language that Karim told them later was Dari. Shop owners and stallholders competed to get them to buy their wares. Karim enjoyed the attention more than they did.

"Here sisters," shouted one in English, "I have the best shawls in Kabul!"

Another yelled, "Buy your dried fruit and nuts here!"

Karim guided them through the bazaar, gently pushing the crowds aside to make a path.

"I will show you the best shops," he said, stopping outside a shop selling leather bags.

The owner was an old man with a shock of white hair. When he saw his visitors, he put down his hookah and got up from a cushion on the floor.

"Please, come in. Welcome. See my bags. I make them all."

The smell of the leather was overpowering. A fan whirled in the corner but the shop still felt hot and smelled like a camel shed. But the bags were works of art. Even Ritu had to admit they were beautiful and soft. They were the colour of fudge.

It didn't take long for Karim to strike a good bargain for two bags – one for Ritu and one for Meena. Harpreet counted out a large pile of afghanis and handed them to Karim who spoke rapidly to the beaming shop owner. They moved onto a shop selling pashmina shawls. Harpreet bought a lovely green one as a gift for her mother. It would keep her warm through the winter, she thought.

Two hours had passed when they decided they had had enough of shopping. The sounds, smell and heat of the bazaar felt overwhelming to them in their jetlagged state, and they were getting hungry.

Karim guided them back to the hotel where he arranged for a meal of freshly baked bread, grilled chicken and vegetable kebabs to be served in their room. After that Harpreet decided they should have a siesta. When they woke nearly four hours later, it was early evening. They rose and washed their faces.

Harpreet rang reception and asked for tea to be brought to their room. In no time, there was a knock on the door.

"Yes. Come in," said Harpreet. Karim came in

carrying a pot of tea, cups and cakes on a tray. He put them down on the table and passed each of them a cup before offering them the plate of cakes.

Karim looked at Harpreet shyly.

"Would madam like to see the views of Kabul from our hotel roof?"

"I have to say my daily prayers, but the girls may be interested. What do you think?" she said to Meena and Ritu.

"Why not?" Ritu said. "Might as well see as much of Kabul as we can. Let's take the tea with us."

Karim looked pleased with himself. He held the door while Meena and Ritu put on their sandals and grabbed the teacups.

"We go in the lift," he said, leading them along the corridor to a lift marked "Staff only".

"Guests are not allowed on the roof normally," he said with a grin.

"So why are we going?" asked Ritu.

"To see my beautiful city," he answered. "I would like to show you."

He summoned the lift by pressing a button. Soon, the doors opened and they got in.

Ritu began to suspect Karim's motives. He appeared to have planned this little adventure in the hope that Harpreet would not come.

The lift stopped. Karim stepped out and they followed.

"Up a few stairs," he said, opening a door to reveal a staircase. At the top there was another door.

"Please follow me carefully. The stairs are narrow," he said.

When they reached the top, he opened the door. When they stepped out, they could not believe their eyes. Kabul spread out before them, surrounded by a circle of mountains. There were many high-rise buildings and numerous examples of beautiful, grand architecture. There was a large green park in the distance, and the sky was a rainbow of kites sailing in the wind. These competed with the sea of television aerials that resembled an army of metal structures on top of houses.

Ritu also saw hundreds more billboards carrying the photograph of the man with the piercing eyes.

"Karim," she asked, "who is the man on the billboards? Is he a local hero or something?"

"He is our President, Nur Mohammad Taraki" Karim said. "He likes his own face. There is a joke in Kabul that he does not own a mirror, hence all the photographs!" He laughed a sarcastic laugh and Ritu guessed he was no fan of the President.

Directly opposite the hotel was another huge billboard advertising a Hindi film. It bore gaudy paintings of two Bollywood actors, Rishi Kapoor and Ranjeeta.

"Look!" said Meena pointing excitedly. "*Laila Majnu*, the Bollywood film."

"Yes!" said Karim. "In Kabul, we love Hindi movies. I go and watch." He looked at Meena shyly. "You look like a film actress," he said.

Meena giggled as Ritu rolled her eyes.

"You think so?"

"Oh yes," he replied. "You are very beautiful. I fall in love with you."

Meena laughed but Ritu felt uncomfortable.

They stared silently at the city for a while.

"You are the older sister, no?" said Karim, addressing Ritu.

"Yes, but only by a year and a half," she said, feeling grumpy. "What of it?"

"Because I ask your permission and make offer."

"I beg your pardon?"

"Pardon? Beg my pardon? I don't understand," Karim replied. "I ask for your sister's hand in marriage. I offer you ten camels."

Ritu looked at him and began laughing.

"What? You have got to be joking!"

"Okay, you drive a hard bargain. I offer twelve camels then."

Meena looked affronted. The smile had vanished from her face.

"Where do you keep your camels in Kabul?" Ritu asked, intrigued.

"They are at my family's house in our village outside Kabul. We own many camels. I work in Kabul to send money to my family."

"Ritu, let's go. He's giving me the creeps."

"Karim, you will have to make a better offer. My sister is not very good at cooking and cleaning but, as you have said yourself, she looks like a film actress. I will need a lot more than twelve camels, and I will need to inspect them first."

Meena whacked Ritu on the arm. "Shut up the both of you – it's not funny!"

"Oh dear – it seems like Meena is not happy with the offer either, Karim. Perhaps we should go downstairs and discuss it with our mother?"

Karim looked alarmed. "We leave it for now – we talk again tomorrow – just the three of us. Okay?"

Ritu paused as though she was considering this. "Okay Karim, I think that's a good plan." She giggled and gave Meena a slight push towards the stairs. Karim followed them down in silence, somewhat deflated.

As the lift reached their floor, Ritu thought that

maybe her mother was right. Mother was fond of saying that men were the same the world over.

V

Neither Ritu nor Meena mentioned the rooftop conversation to Harpreet. They knew their mother too well. Karim kept out of their way for the rest of the evening.

Next morning at quarter past five they were in reception with the other passengers waiting for the bus to take them to the airport.

Karim loitered on the fringes, occasionally throwing glances in their direction but avoiding eye contact.

Meena and Ritu had their new camel bags over their shoulders.

"What lovely bags," said one woman who had been chatting to Harpreet at the hotel the day before.

"Yes, we got them in the bazaar yesterday for a very good price," boasted Harpreet.

"Oh, I wish I had known. I would have come with you. I would love a bag like this," she said pointing at Ritu's bag.

"Karim took us. It was fun."

"How much did you pay?" the woman asked.

"They were very reasonable. Actually the

equivalent of ten pounds for the two."

"Really?" the woman exclaimed. "I wish I could get one. Do you think I have time?"

Harpreet looked at the woman. She was over-weight and wheezy. There was no way she would be able to run to the shop and back in fifteen minutes.

"Maybe…" Harpreet hesitated.

"Yes?" said the woman.

"Maybe one of my daughters can go with Karim and get you one. They are both young and can run fast. They'll be back in no time."

The woman beamed. "Oh, that would be so kind."

Meena and Ritu exchanged glances.

"But Mum," said Ritu, "we'll miss the bus."

"You girls are fast. It will take no time." Harpreet called over to Karim.

"Karim come here, please."

He appeared immediately.

"Can you go with the girls to the bag shop? We need another bag like this one." Harpreet pointed to Ritu's bag. The woman opened her purse and handed over some money.

Meena whispered urgently to Ritu.

"I'm not going with him. You have to go."

"We should both go."

"No way. Anyway you know how slow I run."

This was true. Meena hated running.

Ritu groaned.

"You owe me," she told Meena.

"Actually, you owe me after trying to get me sold off yesterday!"

Ritu took the notes from the woman and walked quickly out the door, followed by Karim.

They ran for about five minutes but when they reached the shop it was shut. Karim hammered his fist on the glass window. The startled shop owner got up from the floor where he was sleeping on a mat. He rubbed the sleep from his eyes. Recognising Karim, he quickly opened the door.

"Welcome," he said.

Karim told him that they needed a bag identical to Ritu's. It was quickly produced.

Ritu handed over the money and they ran back to the hotel where the bus had arrived and passengers were boarding.

Breathlessly, Ritu handed the bag to the woman who began to examine it carefully.

Meena sidled up to her.

"Did he say anything?" she asked.

"Yes, in fact he did. He said that he had reconsidered his offer. And he had realised that an intellectual like me deserved gold, not camels, so we agreed on two twenty-four carat gold bars."

Meena snorted.

"Anyway, can you believe this woman? She is examining the bag as if she has the right to return it!"

Meena laughed.

Harpreet was chatting to Karim. She gave him some notes, which he quickly secreted in the front pocket of his jeans. He helped them with their luggage and, with a big grin on his face, waved them goodbye.

Ritu and Meena watched him from the bus.

"Oh dear. He looks heartbroken," said Ritu, tongue-in-cheek.

"Do you think?" replied Meena, trying to get a better look.

"No."

As the bus started to move, Ritu closed her eyes. It had been an eventful two days. But at least they would be in Amritsar in a few hours. She thought of trying to get a dozen camels through immigration control and smiled.

THE TIGER IN THE TRUNK

I have always known that my mother can be contrary and that she's prone to exaggeration. That is not to say that she makes things up. No, not at all. In fact, she is at pains to point out that it is against her religion to tell lies. However, she asserts that it is part of the makeup of every Indian woman to add *masala* to a story. Nobody wants to hear a tale told without spice, she says.

Here is an example. We went to see the 3D version of the film *The Life of Pi* at our local cinema. When the tiger suddenly appeared in the boat, Ma forgot she was in a packed cinema and started shouting loudly in Punjabi, "Oh my God! A tiger! He will eat them all up now. They will be his dinner. *Bas. Khatum.*

33

Finished." Thankfully the people around us began laughing, but I turned and told her to keep it down just in case we were asked to leave. She looked so funny with her 3D glasses perched on top of her spectacles I had trouble not laughing more.

Later, when we got home, Ma told us the story of the leopard skin that used to lie before the fireplace in our front room. This skin played quite a role in my childhood. You don't see many leopards wandering around in the British Midlands, so I knew that the poor animal once had an existence elsewhere. On a school trip to the local zoo, I saw leopards that bore more than a passing resemblance to the remnants of the poor creature lying flat on the floor of our front room. This convinced me that my parents had kidnapped and killed a leopard from the zoo, and had placed the evidence in clear view in front of our fireplace.

When I confided my concern about my parents' criminality to my older brother, he nearly wet himself laughing.

"Jesus Christ! What an imagination! That leopard skin came from India. How did you think they got it home from the zoo? On the bus? Two adult fares please and one for the leopard! Hah, hah!"

He liked to don the skin when my parents were

out. He pulled it over his head so that the leopard's snarling face masked his own. The rest of the skin, including the beast's straggly tail, covered his back while he made growling noises and chased my sisters and me around the house.

When we got home from seeing *The Life of Pi*, Ma told me that the leopard skin was a gift to her father from his senior British officers. I knew that my grandfather, Major Maninder Singh – or Nanaji as we called him – was an officer in the Indian army during the final years of the British Raj. According to Ma, Nanaji was a fantastic shot and often accompanied his senior officers on shooting expeditions to the foothills of the Himalayas. On one such occasion, Nanaji shot a "tiger".

One of Ma's quirks is that she cannot tell the difference between a lion, a tiger or a leopard. When she refers to the leopard, she always calls it a "tiger". So Ma's story has become "the tale of the tiger in the trunk" which is probably a good thing because "the tale of the leopard in the suitcase" would not quite have the same ring to it.

Nanaji's senior officers were so impressed with his shooting they gave him the leopard skin as a reward. Nanaji was overwhelmed and tried to give it back but the officers insisted that he take it. He felt it was impolite to argue so he accepted.

"But Ma," I cried, "these poor animals face the risk of extinction. Hunting encourages the illegal practice of trade in skins. Was it not wrong to kill?"

"When did you last have a chicken curry?" Ma replied. "And did you enjoy it or not? Nanaji was only following orders, and it is better that the tiger was killed by soldiers than that the soldiers were killed by the tiger."

"I hope neither of us has the misfortune to be reborn a tiger or a leopard," I said.

'I agree," said Ma. "God probably does not like us killing animals, but sometimes these things happen." She sighed. "Maybe," she said, "the tiger was reborn a soldier!"

"Maybe, Ma, but I think if it was given a choice, it would not have chosen to be born a tiger, to be hunted down and shot!"

"Anyway," said Ma, "it is all *kismet*, fate"

Ma told us how she got married at the tender age of sixteen and how Nanaji had included the leopard skin in her dowry. He said that the skin was valuable and he wanted her new in-laws to know he was not a man to be messed with. The daughter of a tiger slayer deserved to be treated with respect.

A few years after their marriage, Pa decided that

a career in the Indian police force was not for him. He applied for a passport and secured a place at a university in the Midlands that he had no intention of studying at. He then relocated to England where he promptly got a job in a foundry in Coventry. He told Ma that he would send for her once he had settled down and bought a house.

Pa was hardworking, and it didn't take him long to buy a terraced house in a cheaper part of town. He sent Ma a letter telling her to arrange for a passport and a ticket to London.

Ma had never travelled abroad in her life. She was excited and nervous at the prospect and she enthusiastically set about getting herself ready to leave India. With Nanaji's assistance she purchased a large trunk, which she filled with things she thought she would need in her new home.

In went a large jar of her mother's homemade pickles, a selection of Indian spices, Ma's Kashmiri shawls, and thick woollen cardigans with the obligatory handful of moth balls. Added to this went all the things Pa had requested, including his thick woollen blanket, his Punjabi embroidered slippers with the curling toes, and his penknife with the sandalwood handle. In no time at all, the trunk was full.

As her departure date approached, Ma emptied and repacked the trunk at every opportunity, each time managing to add more until it would barely shut. On the final day, Nanaji helped her pack. Just as she squeezed in yet one more *salwar kameez*, he noticed the leopard skin was missing.

"Deepi," he said, "where is the tiger skin?"

"Papaji, it's too big to fit in the trunk," Ma replied.

"Oh no! You must take the tiger skin. Those *gora* English people really value tiger skins. It's worth a lot of money. You must take it or you may regret it later."

Despite Ma's protests, Nanaji fetched the leopard skin, calling to her uncles and cousins as he did. "Joga, Shankar, Resham, Kewal! Come here," he bellowed. "We need to help Deepi close the trunk."

As they came running, Nanaji placed the leopard skin on top of Ma's clothes and brought the lid down. There was no way it was going to shut without force so they all pushed down until the padlocks could be secured.

"Whatever you do, don't open it now until you get to your new home," Uncle Joga said with a laugh.

Ma's eyes misted over when she described leaving her family. Nanaji and Uncle Joga accompanied her to Delhi airport. She started crying as soon as she left the village and did not stop until the plane took off.

It was 1956 and she was one of two Indian passengers on the flight to London. The other was a teacher from Hoshiarpur who had been to London before. Helpfully, the airline had put him in the seat next to her. She was grateful for this as her English was limited, and she was feeling worried. The teacher was courteous, and they exchanged pleasantries until Ma fell into a restless sleep.

When she filed off the flight at Heathrow Airport, she didn't know which way to walk or what she was supposed to do, but the kind teacher accompanied her to the passport desk and then into the baggage area. Without having to be asked, he helped her with her trunk. He gasped with surprise when he felt the weight. "What have you got in there, sister?" he asked. "Not your entire village, I hope." She laughed as they dragged the trunk through the baggage area.

Here she was stopped by a young official in uniform. He asked if he could take a look inside the trunk. The teacher reassured her in Punjabi that this was not unusual and she should allow the man to take a look. It took the man and the teacher all their strength to haul the trunk onto the counter. Ma was getting anxious as she noticed a number of other men in uniform watching.

The teacher helped unfasten the belts that circled

the trunk. Ma then, fumbling, opened the padlock with the key. The trunk burst open and the leopard skin leapt out onto the table, where it bounced a few times before landing on the floor and sliding gradually to a halt. It was as if it had been waiting to be freed after days of captivity squashed in with everything else Ma had managed to cram into the trunk.

The young official gave a cry and jumped backwards as the leopard shot out of the trunk.

"Blimey!" another shouted. "She's got a tiger in the trunk!"

This is how Ma triggered a security alert at Heathrow airport. A bevy of officers materialised when the shout went up, but when everyone realised there was no live tiger to be contained, much relief and laughter followed. Ma was in her element. With the assistance of the teacher who translated for her, she explained to the officials how Nanaji acquired the skin and how it ended up in her trunk. No doubt the story was told with a generous sprinkling of spices.

It still amazes me that Ma was allowed to proceed with the leopard skin, but she says there were no restrictions in those days. Sadly, the leopard skin in question has long gone. When Ma and Pa returned to India some years later, it was bequeathed to Mr Smith, the cobbler who had a shop on the corner of our street in Coventry. He was delighted and I think he turned it into a handbag or two.

After I heard the story from Ma, I told her that I felt sad for the leopard. Had I known then what I know now, I would have smuggled it into my suitcase and taken it back to its home in the Himalayas for a burial.

Ma told me to stop being silly. "You can't go around with tiger skins in your luggage," she said gleefully. "You can be imprisoned for that kind of thing!"

The Indian Firecracker

Auntie Gita sat on the sofa wiping away her tears with the end of her *dupatta*. Ma sat next to her, holding Auntie Gita's other hand, with a concerned look on her face.

"Why would she do this, *Bhenji*?" Auntie Gita stuttered between sobs. *Bhenji* meant "older sister" in Punjabi and this is how Auntie Gita related to Ma.

Auntie Gita was a widow. She lived nearby in a small terraced house which was not that dissimilar to our own. It backed onto a railway line, which made it less desirable as it shook every time a train passed by. Ma and Auntie Gita met in the park soon after she moved into the neighbourhood. That was six years ago. Since then the two had become good friends.

Auntie Gita arrived in the UK in the mid-1960s with her husband, Rahul, and their two children Rakesh and Seema. A year later, when she was pregnant with her third child, Rahul, at the age of only thirty-six, died from a heart attack. Rahul had been a softly spoken man with a love of Urdu poetry and was a devoted husband and father.

Satish was born a few months later. Auntie Gita's health was not great. On receiving the news of Rahul's death she suffered a stroke, and consequently now had difficulty walking on her right leg and impaired vision in one eye. It was clear that Rahul had been the love of her life and something in her had died with him.

Seema once showed me a photograph of her parents taken soon after they were married. They looked so happy and beautiful like Hollywood movie stars. I cannot ever recall seeing Auntie Gita laugh, though on the rare occasions she smiled, her face lit up.

Ma was protective towards Auntie Gita. She helped her with jobs around the house and often sent my brothers, Jas and Sunny, who were older than Auntie's children, to help dig her garden or assist her children with their homework.

Papa never lingered when Auntie Gita visited

our home. He would greet her, ask after her health and that of her children, then go and do something in the other room. Later, after she had gone, Ma would tell Papa about Auntie Gita's problems. He would listen carefully and was supportive. I wondered what he would say after hearing about Auntie Gita's latest predicament.

"I don't know, Gita,' said Ma. "I don't know why she would do such a thing. But it has to stop."

"How?" wailed Auntie Gita. "Haven't I suffered enough without her going around ruining my reputation saying I am a loose woman with a loose daughter?"

Ma's eyebrows twitched. Her eyes flashed. I knew she was angry. Her temper was something to behold. Ma defied every stereotype about Asian women being passive. Anybody who knew how to read the signals ran for cover when her eyebrows began twitching.

"That's it," said Ma, getting up from the sofa and putting on her shoes. "We are going to pay that interfering witch a visit."

Auntie Gita looked up with surprise. "What now, *Bhenji*? What if she has visitors, or her husband is at home?"

"So what?" replied Ma. "I am going to sort her out once and for all. She will never raise her eyes in front of you again, never mind say anything about you. All the better if her good-for-nothing husband is home. He will get a tongue-lashing too!"

Then, seeing Auntie Gita's worried face, she added softly, "Don't worry, Gita. You won't have to do anything. Leave it to me. Come on."

I got up from the carpet where I had been lying listening to the conversation. Without being asked to join them, I quickly put on my shoes. I wasn't going to miss this! My younger sister, Inder, was in the other room watching TV. I ran in and told her that Ma was off to sort out Bimla for gossiping about Auntie Gita. I got her attention straight away and saw her eyes light up with excitement. She turned off the television and scrambled to her feet.

"Come on, quick!" Ma was already out of the front door. We ran to join them. Ma was too busy chatting to Auntie Gita to notice us following. I knew she would send us home if she spied us, so we kept quiet.

Bimla lived in the next street and it was not long before Ma and Gita stood outside the terraced house with its blue door.

Ma marched forward and rang the doorbell. There was no answer. Ma banged on the door and shouted "Oy! Bimla! Come out here, you interfering witch!"

Still no answer. Auntie Gita, Inder and I watched from a few feet away. Auntie Gita looked worried and tugged nervously at the ends of her *dupatta*. Ma got angrier. "She is home. I can tell," she said, before striding to the window and rapping it loudly.

"Come out, you shameless woman or I'm going to break down your door!"

I noticed that some of Bimla's neighbours had come out to see what all the commotion was about. They stood watching this deranged Asian woman shouting in a language they could not understand. Nobody called the police.

Ma looked at the upstairs window and caught a glimpse of Bimla hiding behind the curtain.

"Hey you! The biggest liar in the world. Come out here and show your face. See if I don't beat you black and blue in return. My shoe has your name already printed on it."

It was clear Bimla was not going to come out. I didn't blame her. Ma was not making empty threats. I wondered about Ma's strategy. If I were in Bimla's shoes, the promise of a good thrashing was a major disincentive to emerge from the relative safety of my home.

Auntie Gita moved forward and held Ma's arm. "Let's go. She is not coming out. I think she's got the message though. The children will need their dinner soon. Let's go home."

Ma refused to leave without one last attempt. She kicked the door and shouted, "Don't let me catch you walking past my house or anywhere near Gita's house, or God be my witness, I will thrash you."

With that, she turned and began walking home. During the exchange, Inder and I swung on the garden gate. Now we jumped off and ran behind Ma and Auntie Gita, skipping to keep up.

A few doors down, in the garden of a house, stood a handsome young man wearing flared jeans and a tight red tee shirt. He whistled as Ma walked past. "Wow! You go girl! She must have really pissed you off. Been messing with your fella, has she?"

Ma glared at him. He gave her a broad smile and winked suggestively.

"*Badmaash*! Hoodlum!" Ma muttered as Auntie Gita pulled her *dupatta* tightly around her head.

"Steady, tiger," said the man. "I may be a bad-arse but I know a firecracker when I see one!" He laughed and winked again at Inder and me. Inder grinned back as I pulled her alongside me.

Ma tutted loudly and quickened her pace. "*Besharam*. Shameless."

The area we lived in was home to many Asian

and Irish immigrants. It was not uncommon to see people arguing loudly in the street or children receiving a scolding and a clip around the ear from a neighbour with everybody else watching or providing a running commentary.

Later, I heard Ma telling Papa what happened. He began laughing.

"I'm glad she didn't come out," he said. "She will run the other way if she ever sees you in the street or park."

Next day, Papa as usual was at work. He was a bus driver for the city corporation, as was Bimla's husband, Malkit. Papa was in the drivers' room looking at the staff notice board to see what shift he was on, when he heard somebody say, "*Jeldara*! Listen, I need to talk to you."

Papa looked at Malkit suspiciously. "What do you want?" he asked.

"It's about your wife. She came over to my house yesterday and threatened my wife. Now she is too frightened to leave the house. You need to control your missus. She is out of control. No woman should be so bold."

Papa looked at Malkit with contempt before replying, "No, you listen to me. Nobody controls my wife. Before you go around saying I should control my wife, look to your own. You need to have a word with her. It is not wise to spread malicious rumours about decent women."

"This is the problem with your kind," retorted Malkit. "You may be aristocracy in India but here you are nothing! You are no better than me."

Papa's patience was running out.

"I am better than you, *bewakoof!* Idiots like you treat women like second class citizens. Learn some respect!"

Malkit tried to interrupt but Papa wouldn't let him. "If your wife has any sense, she will stay out of my wife's way. And you stay out of my way. Now, *duffa ho*! Clear off!" He pushed past Malkit and walked out the room.

When Papa related the exchange to Ma, she laughed.

"And there was me thinking that my years of lecturing you about women's rights were wasted."

"I blame my aristocratic parents for finding me a bold wife," Papa said mournfully while trying not to laugh.

Some months later, Ma and I were walking through the park.

"Hello, darling,' said a male voice. "Well, if it isn't the Indian firecracker, herself."

We turned to see a young man wearing jeans and a black tee shirt. He grinned. It took me a few seconds to recognise him as the man in the garden near Bimla's house.

Ma grabbed my arm and pulled me towards her like a barrier.

"*Jaldi, chal*! Quickly, move!" she hissed.

"It's okay, flower. Just being friendly. Did you know your mate and her fella have sold up and moved on?"

Ma looked at him, puzzled.

"You remember? The girl that was after your fella?"

The penny dropped. Ma looked relieved.

"Oh, thank you. I didn't know."

"My pleasure. Now, what about joining me for a drink sometime?"

I looked at Ma's face. To my astonishment, she was smiling.

"No, I don't think my husband would approve. But maybe..." she hesitated.

The man raised his eyebrows expectantly.

"But maybe what?" he asked.

"Maybe we could all join you. I mean, my husband, me and our five kids?"

The man looked startled.

"Oh well, never mind," he said, recovering himself. "But what about your friend? You know, the mysterious, shy-looking, exotic one who was with you that day?"

He meant Auntie Gita.

Shaking her head, Ma laughed. Without answering, she strode off, pulling me close.

I looked back over my shoulder at the man. He stood watching us with a big grin on his face. His sky blue eyes met mine and he winked mischievously. I smiled back then turned away and clasped Ma's hand.

I matched her confident strides even though my short legs struggled to keep up with her. It probably made me look comical but I didn't care. It felt good being the daughter of an Indian firecracker.

Whisky and Sauna

As he drove through the slow-moving traffic, Jas listened to his mother, Sukhvir. She always looks well groomed, he thought, looking at her hair neatly tied back in a ponytail and her matching green cardigan, *salwar kameez* and scarf.

"Jas," she said, "you can pick me up at six o'clock from Auntie Deeshi's house. I'll come outside, so no need to call me."

"Mum," he said as he looked across at her, smiling, "I'll be there. Don't worry."

He glanced at his mother's face. She always looked happy on her visits to her friend Deeshi's house. They had been best friends for over twenty years. Although they had grown up with entirely different backgrounds, they shared many things in life.

"Your mother and I are soul sisters," Deeshi would say. "We were blood sisters in a previous life."

Jas thought this was very unlikely. He knew that his mother came from a long line of landowners whereas Deeshi was from the travelling community. They were unlikely friends, but the United Kingdom did funny things to entrenched Indian stereotypes. He never voiced these thoughts as he knew his mother would scold him. She did not approve of the caste system or snobbery.

Today was the day for Sukhvir and Deeshi's visit to the sauna and some of Deeshi's female relatives were joining them. Jas was curious about these visits as he noticed that his mother always looked forward to them but rarely told him what they discussed or why she enjoyed them so much.

Sukhvir looked back at her son. She knew he was curious about her visits to the sauna, but she wasn't going to tell him any more than he needed to know. Sauna days were special days spent with her women friends and were not to be discussed with men. Her upbringing as an Asian woman meant that she did not feel comfortable being questioned by her son on such matters.

They arrived at Deeshi's house. She was standing in the doorway surrounded by plastic bags. Her face broke into an enormous smile when she saw them. She moved towards the car as Jas got out and opened the door for his mother. He watched as the two women warmly embraced and exchanged greetings.

Deeshi then turned to him and said, "Hello Jas. How is your family? Work going well?"

"All well, Auntie, thanks. I'll be back to pick up mum at six o'clock. Any problems, call me. Have a nice time. See you later." As he drove away, he looked in his driver's mirror and saw them laughing.

"Did you remember to bring your towel, *Bhenji*?" Deeshi asked. "Otherwise I have spare ones in the house."

"All here," replied Sukhvir, pointing to her bag, "and I brought some lime pickle that I made just the other day."

"Good, let's go," said Deeshi. She walked back to the doorway and shouted down the hallway, "Come on, girls. Hurry. Auntie is here and it is time to go."

Three women emerged from the house wearing brightly coloured and heavily embroidered *salwar kameezes*, and wearing generous amounts of gold jewellery. They hugged Sukhvir warmly.

"Gagan can drive," said Deeshi as they piled into a red estate. Deeshi sat in front with Gagan, her daughter, whilst Sukhvir squeezed in the back between Shan, Deeshi's sister-in-law, and Rani, Deeshi's daughter-in-law.

The public baths and sauna were housed in a large building owned by the local council and situated on the seafront with a beautiful vista.

Passers-by looked on with amusement as they piled out of the car trailing their bags with them. Giggling, they entered the lobby of the building. There were two female attendants at the kiosk.

"Usual, girls?" asked the older attendant.

"Usual," replied Shan with a smile. "Five for a private room please."

The woman gave her a key and a receipt.

"Why do they want a private room?" the younger attendant asked when Sukhvir and her friends were out of earshot.

"I think it's their religion. They don't like undressing in the communal rooms or displaying their flesh to strangers in the sauna."

"Aah – that makes sense."

Safely in the dressing room, the women undressed and put their clothes and plastic bags into the lockers provided.

"Did you bring the you-know-what?" Sukhvir asked Deeshi as she undressed. Deeshi lifted her *kurta* and pointed to the pockets sewn into the inside. She extracted a whisky flask.

"Here is our friend," she laughed.

After wrapping the towels around themselves the five women headed into the sauna and spread themselves out, like seals on the beach, on the wooden benches running round the sides of the room. The heat was intense and soon they were all sweating profusely and fanning themselves. After about fifteen minutes, they had had enough.

"Let's go and relax in the other room," said Deeshi.

They returned to the dressing room, which had a row of showers at the back. As the cold water crashed down on their hot skin they squealed. Then began the ritual of drying each other's backs and wrapping themselves in a fresh set of dry towels.

Shan and Gagan began emptying the plastic bags. They took out packets wrapped in tin foil, Tupperware containers, paper plates, plastic knives and forks, and paper cups. Rani handed out plates and cutlery whilst Deeshi opened the containers and unwrapped the tin foil parcels.

"Auntie, what shall I give you?" asked Gagan.

"Just one *paratha* and some potato curry for now," replied Sukhvir. "And here's the lime pickle and some *samosas*," she said, removing a jar and a plastic box from her bag.

Gagan handed her the food whilst Deeshi opened the whisky flask and poured shots into their five paper cups. She added some water from a bottle to each and handed them around.

When everyone had one she said, "*Shabash*. Good. Here is to good health," and with a laugh knocked back the contents. The others followed and Deeshi refilled the cups.

Soon they were chatting, laughing and eating, oblivious to the sign on the wall above their heads which said, "No eating or drinking." As the whisky took effect, their voices became louder and their talk more raucous.

"Auntie," said Gagan, "tell us that story about when you went to the Canaries."

Sukhvir laughed. "That story," she said. "You want to hear it again?"

"Yes, yes," the others chorused.

"It was about five years ago," Sukhvir began. "For the New Year, my middle daughter took me on holiday to the Canaries. 'Mum', she said, 'It will be nice and warm and sunny. It will be good for you'. So we went and she was right. It was very hot. On the second day of our holiday, Reena said to me, 'Mum, let's go down to the beach. It will be nice and cool with a sea breeze.'

"So I agreed and we made our way down from the apartment to the beach. On our way, we passed a man standing at a bus stop on the opposite side of the road. This was by the track we had started to take to walk down to the beach. He looked across at us, lowered his trousers, turned and very deliberately flashed his bare bottom at us. Then, laughing, he pulled up his trousers and shouted something at us in Spanish while pointing at the beach. Reena and I looked at each other in astonishment. She was really annoyed, but I told her to ignore him, as he was probably mad. We continued walking down to the beach where we noticed large circular dugouts in the sand with seating around the edges. They looked really comfortable so we lowered ourselves into one and sat on the seats. We must have looked like meerkats with our heads above the parapet looking across the sandy beach."

Sukhvir's audience was chuckling. They had heard the story before, but Sukhvir had a way of telling it that always made it sound fresh and funny.

She took a slug of whisky from her cup then went on. "We'd taken refreshments and books with us, so we settled down and started reading. I put on my sunglasses and covered my head with my scarf. Reena wore a baseball cap and put her feet up on the seat. After a while, we heard male voices nearby. Peering over the top of the dugout we saw, a few feet away from us, two men. Neither wearing a stitch! Absolutely naked, I tell you!"

The women started to laugh. "*Bhenji*, what did you do?" asked Shan.

"Nothing at first," said Sukhvir. "I couldn't believe my eyes and didn't know where to look. Here we were minding our own business and these two *gora* were looking straight at us, grinning like monkeys! Then one of them said, '*Guten tag*' and something else in German that we didn't understand. Reena tried to look away and said, 'We don't speak German. We're English,' to which he replied, 'Oh, English! Good morning ladies. Nice day for it.' I had lowered my eyes and did not reply. When I next looked up, all I could see were four brown, hairy bum-cheeks walking away from us!"

The four women listening were now rolling with laughter. Sukhvir was having difficulty continuing because she was laughing so much herself.

Gagan said, "Auntie, so they were wearing nothing?"

Sukhvir replied, "Oh, they had lovely designed hankies on their heads. Nice patterns, and possibly made of silk, I remember."

The women roared with laughter and tears fell down their cheeks.

"Wait, wait," said Sukhvir, "there's more. I was so surprised I said to Reena, 'Let's go home now. I've seen enough bare bums for one day.' As we walked back Reena kept saying, 'Mum, that was terrible! What were they doing with no clothes on? And that other man flashing his bum? We should report them to the police.' I nodded in agreement, trying all the time not to laugh. Then we saw a sign. I don't know how we missed it on the way in. It said 'Nudist beach. Adults only.' If I'd known in advance I would have taken my camera!"

The women grew hysterical.

"Of course it all made sense then. The man at the bus stop must have thought we too were nudists on our way to join in!"

"I wish I'd been there," said Deeshi. "Yes, next time take me too," said Shan. "You don't get visions like that on beaches here. So cold your teeth would be chattering!"

They refreshed their paper cups with whisky and knocked it back.

....

At six o'clock, Jas opened the passenger door for his mother. She stumbled as she got in. "You okay, Mum?" he said, grabbing her arm to steady her.

"Fine, fine," she said. "Foot slipped, that's all."

As she spoke, he caught a whiff of green cardamoms. And… was that a hint of whisky he could smell on his mother's breath? No, it couldn't be. His mother didn't drink.

He got in and put the car into gear. Deeshi stood in the doorway of her house smiling and waving as they drove off.

"Have a good time, Mum?" he enquired.

"Yes, we had a nice time," Sukhvir replied, "But I'm feeling a bit tired now." Her head had begun to throb. Deeshi pours the drinks too strong, she thought, as she closed her eyes. Next time, she should add more water.

Jas glanced at her curiously. He turned on the radio and drove her home.

THE DANCING MAHARANI

Gurpreet laughed as she danced. She took slow steps between each twirl, her hands clapping to the rhythm, her head moving gently from side to side as she sang along to the music. She loved dancing. Here she was, as an old woman, dancing before an attentive audience on her birthday.

If the truth were told she did not know her real age, although she had a rough idea based on events that had occurred at the time. She knew that few people of her generation born in India were sure of their actual birth date. Anyway, that was all irrelevant today as her family had organised a party to celebrate her reaching her ninth decade. Through the expansive hotel window she could see the sparkling lights of London reflected in the Thames.

Her eyes shone as her son and grandson reached out and grasped her hands gently and lifted them into the air. Her pink *salwar kameez* was billowing and swishing as she moved, and she knew all eyes were on her. Her younger companions were doing the energetic moves of the *Bhangra*, the dance celebrating the harvest, but she preferred the *Gidda*, the traditional Punjabi folk women's dance, with its slow and suggestive moves.

Who would believe it? Here she was dancing to her heart's content, encouraged, applauded and accompanied by loud whistles before a gathering of men and women. Men who were not related to her. Men and women who were not of her caste, faith, colour or nationality. She could not quite believe it herself. Her daughters and granddaughters joined the dancing. She looked at them, her smile becoming broader. No one to judge any of them.

She knew how it worked: videos and photos would be taken and then shared to an even wider audience on Facebook and other social media.

She was always making her children and grandchildren laugh. "Don't be putting my face on Face to Face," she would tell them, pretending to be mortified. This made them roar with laughter.

"It's Facebook, Granny, not Face to Face," her youngest granddaughter would say. "And anyway, the world deserves to see my nana's radiant face!"

At this, she would give her granddaughter a big hug and kiss.

If only Resham, her mother-in-law, could see her now. And suddenly her mind flashed back to when she was just sixteen years old, a full sixty-four years earlier. She was newly married. Her eyes taking in everything all around her. A new home and husband, new in-laws, everything unknown.

She remembered what her mother had said to her before she got married: "Be humble and obedient. Don't answer back. Most importantly, never question your mother-in-law. She is your mother now." This struck her as odd. How could anybody take her mother's place? Even if she did think this was possible, she was used to arguing with her mother so why could she not question her mother-in-law too?

"This is your problem," her mother had replied irritably. "Your father has spoilt you and now you question too much. You need to learn to keep quiet. Girls from good families don't question their elders."

Later that evening she recounted the conversation to her father. He laughed and stroked her face. "You are my *noor*," he said, "my jewel. Of course, your mother-in-law can never replace your mother. All your mother was doing was trying to reassure you, so you don't miss us too much!" He laughed even more loudly but she could see his eyes were clouded over with sadness.

Gurpreet remembered the day as if it were yesterday. She had been very excited as she was going to a wedding in the village with Resham and Paro, Gurpreet's new sister-in-law. She had not ventured out much since her marriage, and her mother-in-law's announcement that she was to get ready and accompany her and Paro came as a big surprise. She remembered the tight lanes they had had to negotiate to reach the wedding house. They were muddy, uneven and treacherous after a recent rainstorm, and their task was made even trickier because they were shrouded in *chadors* – sheets which covered their bodies and faces. She could barely see in front of her but she could see Resham's feet as she looked down, so she used them to guide her.

Resham had such beautiful feet, she thought. They were long and thin and perfectly formed. Gurpreet thought Resham was still very beautiful beneath the sheet, which covered her completely and gave nothing away. She had fair, smooth skin, blue eyes with sharp features, and silky black hair that was tied into a long plait which snaked down her spine to her waist. She was tall and walked gracefully. Paro had not inherited her mother's features and in fact was quite the opposite. She had a stout, short figure with a hint of a moustache and bushy, thick eyebrows. Gurpreet had first set eyes upon her husband on her wedding day, and now she guiltily remembered her relief at discovering that he was handsome and tall like his mother.

The trio were greeted warmly at the wedding house. A fuss had been made as they entered and discarded their *chadors*. People smiled and looked down when her mother- in-law addressed them.

"We are so honoured that you came," said Bakshi, the mother of the groom. "Welcome to our house. So lovely that you brought your new daughter-in-law. She is very beautiful."

At this Gurpreet blushed. She felt all eyes were suddenly on her and her red *salwar kameez*, embroidered with gold thread that glistened when she moved.

Resham did not look at her as she replied, "We are happy. All in God's hands."

Gurpreet realised with surprise that her mother-in-law was like a goddess; people were bashful and servile when she spoke to them. This was something she had not expected. It had never been like this at home where her parents kept their front gate open all day and consequently had a constant flow of visitors. People seeking advice or help. They all knew that they would not be turned away empty-handed: some sought loans of sugar, rice, flour or even money. Gurpreet's parents were generous and sociable, unlike her in-laws.

Bakshi led them into a room which was full of chattering women and girls. Most sat on the floor or stood at the side. As they entered, the chatter became subdued. Three chairs were brought in and they were invited to sit. A table appeared and was placed in front of them with drinks and snacks. She noticed that neither Resham nor Paro ate, although they sipped at their tea from time to time. Gurpreet eyed the snacks wistfully but she lacked the courage to take some.

After a few minutes, the chatter had returned to its original volume. Gurpreet surveyed the room and noticed that one of the women sitting on the floor held a small drum between her knees. Another had a spoon. They began singing folk songs. The one with the spoon began tapping it on the side of the drum in time to the singing. The songs were familiar to Gurpreet; she had heard and sung many of them herself in her own village. The women laughed as they sang. Some of the older women started dancing. They were clapping and moving around the room.

She smiled as she watched them dance, glancing sideways at Resham and Paro, who were looking on with expressionless faces. Others joined the dancing women. They were laughing and Gurpreet started to tap her feet and clap. The music became louder and the songs more raucous.

One of the older women came up to them and said, "Come. Please dance".

Resham and Paro declined but Gurpreet could not resist. She rose from the chair, pushing the table to the side, and started moving around the room, clapping and singing and smiling broadly. Her scarf had fallen from her shoulders and her hair moved like a wave around her. She was a blur of red and gold, transported to another world. The world of another village where her cousins and aunts and male relatives danced with her.

The song finished. Breathless and laughing, she glanced over to Resham who was glaring at her. Paro sat with her mouth open in astonishment. Resham indicated with her eyes that Gurpreet should sit. She knew that she had done something seriously wrong.

The look said it all. Lowering her eyes, she sat down.

Resham bent towards her and whispered into Gurpreet's ear. "In this family we do not dance," she hissed. "We pay whores and dancing girls to do that. We certainly do not dance in public. What were you thinking? Did your parents not teach you anything?"

The words shocked her and tears stung her eyes. She felt a rush of anger, confusion, shame and fear, and wished she could disappear. The other women continued to dance and sing without her. She sensed that they knew better than to incur Resham's wrath having witnessed the exchange, even though they hadn't heard the words.

After some time Resham arose, indicating that she had suffered enough. Not a word passed between them as they walked back through the lanes. Upon reaching home, Resham went to lie down saying that she had a headache. Gurpreet also went to her bedroom. She was worried what would happen when her husband was told what she had done. She knew there would be an argument as he didn't approve of music. When they had first arrived at her husband's house, she had been struck by the silence which was only interrupted when the local *gurdwara* had the loudspeaker on for morning and evening prayers.

Gurpreet had loved listening to the radio at home. Her in-laws had a radio but the only person who appeared to have any say in what they listened to was her father-in-law. And he only seemed interested in the news. Paro usually sneaked into her room on the rare occasions when Resham was out.

"Quick, let's put the radio on," Paro would say and like a pair of naughty schoolgirls they would giggle as they crept into the dining room where the radio was kept.

They would tune it in to a channel playing film songs and dance around the room. So it was not true, women did dance in this house! She now thought with horror about the consequences if they had been caught.

As she lay on the bed, Gurpreet missed her family more than ever. She wondered why her parents had married her into such a household. Most of all, she felt sad at the prospect of never dancing again, or at least not while she lived in her husband's village.

Later she would reflect on that day. Her husband had not said a word to her about it and she often wondered if Resham had even mentioned it to him. She would never know as he was now dead, and so were Resham and Paro. One thing was for sure, she never did dance in that house again. Paro no longer suggested that they play the radio when Resham went out. Perhaps she too had realised that the penalty for this particular misdemeanour would be too much to bear.

Now though, Gurpreet was surrounded by young men and women. Clapping, gyrating their hips and dancing energetically. She was in the middle, swirling gently and singing.

The song was a favourite at weddings and parties. "Dance, young girl, dance, young girl!" the male vocalist sang in Punjabi. Gurpreet saw that a trolley holding a cake had been wheeled in. It was a huge cake covered in eighty candles. She blew them all out in one breath. A glass of champagne was pressed into her hand by her granddaughter.

"Happy birthday, Grandma! You are the Dancing Maharani, the Dancing Queen."

Gurpreet laughed as she took a large mouthful of champagne. If only her mother-in-law could see her now. Dancing, drinking, and cavorting with men and women, and not struck down dead yet. Resham was wrong. She would dance forever. The Dancing Maharani.

DAISY

Daisy was missing. She was last seen at eleven o'clock that morning when Ram had moved her from the rear of the house to the shade at the front to avoid the searing sun. He had chopped up some freshly cut greens and, after giving her a cool refreshing shower with the hosepipe, he filled her trough.

Daisy had seemed contented enough. As she casually chomped through the greens, she flicked her tail over her back to remove the flies that dared to land on her. Ram had then gone off to the bazaar nearby to shop for the vegetables and fruit that Rekha, his employer, had asked him to get.

At twelve noon, Ram decided to weed the front garden. As he passed the spot where he had tethered

Daisy to the iron post with rope to prevent her from wandering off, he noticed she had gone.

Daisy was not a curious or adventurous buffalo. In fact, Ram thought she was the most placid buffalo he had ever cared for. She was happy just to meander round the large garden. Sometimes, Ram let her graze in the empty plot of land that lay adjacent to the house. He never worried about her as she was not the kind of animal to get up to mischief. She was the exact opposite of that jersey cow, Shanti, owned by Bibiji's father, who delighted in kicking like a prize bull if given half a chance. He rubbed his leg at the memory of receiving a painful kick from one of her well-aimed hooves once when he had been asked to look after her.

Ram searched the garden, front and back. He jumped on to the wall and peered into the empty plot, but there was no sign of her. The gate was open so it was possible that Daisy had wandered down the road. He looked up and down the empty street but she was not there. He began to grow anxious and felt apprehensive about telling Bibiji the bad news. Bibiji would not react well, this he knew from experience. But he knew things would get a lot worse if he did not tell her.

He ran to the kitchen where Rekha was chopping vegetables for the lunchtime curry.

"Bibiji! Bibiji!" he cried.

"What is it?" Rekha asked without lifting her head.

"It's Daisy. She's gone."

"Gone? Gone where? Have you looked for her?"

"Bibiji, I have searched everywhere. I have looked in the street and in the empty plot but she is not there. She has gone."

Rekha looked at Ram in disbelief, then put down the knife and wiped her hands on the towel.

"Daisy is a buffalo. She is not a cheetah capable of running miles. She cannot be far. Where is Sunny?"

"I don't know, Bibiji".

"Sunny!" she shouted. "Where are you? Come quick. Daisy has gone."

Sunny, her son, appeared at the door with a book in his hand.

"Ma, can't you see I am studying? I have an exam tomorrow."

Rekha gave him one of her "don't mess with me" looks.

"Exams can wait. We need to find Daisy. Go on the scooter now and see if you can find her. She can't have gone far. Ram, you go too. Search everywhere."

Sunny could see that his mother was getting anxious and agitated.

"It's okay, Ma. Don't worry. Daisy does not run. She is the slowest animal on the planet. We will find her."

He left his book on a chair on the verandah and walked quickly over to the scooter which stood with its key in the ignition.

"Ram, you go towards the market and I will go towards the bus station."

Rekha walked to the gate and watched them go. She pulled her *dupatta* nervously around her neck. Where had Daisy disappeared to? And who had left the front gate open? Ram would need a good talking to.

Half an hour passed as she fretted in the kitchen. She heard the sound of the scooter returning, so she quickly took the curry off the gas stove, turned off the heat and went outside.

Sunny and Ram were standing together on the verandah looking worried. There was no sign of Daisy.

"So, where is she?" said Rekha looking up and down the driveway.

"No sign of her, Ma. I think she has been kidnapped."

"Don't be ridiculous," Rekha snapped. "She is a buffalo, not the Kohinoor diamond. We need to find her before your Papa gets home else all hell will break loose."

Gurdial, Rekha's husband, had a temper. He got wound up at the slightest thing. Rekha was right – Sunny knew Daisy had to be found before his father got home.

Suddenly Rekha had a thought. She ran inside and quickly changed her clothes and grabbed her handbag.

"Sunny, turn the scooter around. Take me to the Old Bazaar to see Panditji. He will know where Daisy is."

Sunny rolled his eyes and looked at Ram, who was staring at Rekha with a puzzled look on his face.

Panditji was an elderly man who lived in the oldest part of the city in a run-down house, accessible only through narrow, muddied lanes. He advised his clients on every aspect of their lives, and was very popular as he had built up a reputation for solving most problems, however trivial. Indians love astrologers and Panditji was no exception. He was never short of customers but he was not a greedy man. He did not ask for money but left donations to the discretion of his customers. They, in turn, rewarded him handsomely for his services.

Sunny stopped the scooter outside Panditji's

house. Rekha told him to wait as she made her way inside. As she stepped through the ornate and heavy wooden door, Panditji's assistant, Gopal, greeted her with his hands clasped together.

"*Namaste*, Rekha sister," he said, "Panditji is through here. Please come." Rekha returned the greeting and followed Gopal into the room where she could see Panditji sitting cross-legged on the floor. He wore a white *kurta* pyjama and a white turban on his head.

As he looked up and saw her, he smiled and put his hands together in greeting indicating that she should sit down in front of him. The other men and women in the room, having witnessed the exchange, made room for her, sensing that Rekha was an important guest who took priority.

Rekha sat down and covered her head with her *dupatta*, which had slipped off.

"*Namaste*, Rekhaji," he said in his kindly voice. "How are you? All well at home I trust?"

"Panditji, thank you. It was all well at home until a problem which has just arisen this morning."

Rekha sensed that she had an avid audience as the men and women around her leaned in to hear the details. She was reminded that there was no concept of privacy in India. It was as though everybody felt they had the right to eavesdrop and express an opinion whether it was sought or not.

"It's our Daisy, Panditji. She has gone missing. We have looked everywhere but she is not to be found. You know my husband. He has a short fuse. We have to find Daisy before he returns from work this evening."

Panditji listened carefully and nodded.

"I understand the problem, Rekhaji. And Daisy, she is one of your lovely children, no?"

"Oh, no," laughed Rekha "Daisy is our buffalo, but she is like family."

Panditji looked surprised but managed to quickly compose himself. He leaned forward and smiled. From his previous encounters with Rekha, he had formed the view that she was a bit eccentric. He enjoyed her visits as, unlike his other clients, she did not bring him mundane problems. The family were quite unusual. They had returned from England having left India a long time previously, and he had come to the conclusion that this had affected their behaviour. Living in such a cold climate with English people for such a long time would have an effect on any Indian surely?

"Oh," he said, "Daisy is a buffalo! Now let me think." He closed his eyes and sat silently for a few minutes.

Rekha glanced at her watch hoping Panditji would not see her. It was already over two hours since Daisy had gone missing.

As if he had read her mind, at that moment Panditji opened his eyes. Speaking calmly he said, "Time is ticking on. Daisy is grazing on Ladowali Road. She is with a herd of buffalos but you will recognise her from the distinct collar that you have put around her neck. You will recognise her immediately and she will recognise you."

Rekha gasped with relief and surprise, as did the audience. How did Panditji know that Daisy was wearing a collar that her daughter, Nishi, had made from a remnant piece of cotton that bore a flower pattern?

"Thank you, Panditji! You are a Saint. I knew you would know! You must excuse me. I must go immediately and bring Daisy home," said Rekha as she got to her feet.

Panditji smiled as he put his hands together and bade her farewell.

On her way out, Rekha extracted a few notes from her handbag and pressed them into Gopal's hand.

Gopal touched his forehead with the notes and put them in his pocket.

Sunny was sitting on the scooter drinking a bottle of coke. When he saw Rekha emerge from the house, he passed the bottle over to a young boy who stood next to him and who had put his hand out to receive it. Sunny knew that the boy would get a few paisa for the bottle from the local shopkeeper.

"Sunny, drop me off at home and take Ram with you. Panditji says that Daisy is in Ladowali Road with a herd of buffalos. You will recognise her from the collar that Nishi made."

Sunny looked puzzled but he did what his mother asked. As they made their way through the tight lanes, Rekha was grateful she had not removed the collar from Daisy's neck as she had originally planned to do when Nishi first placed it there, thinking that it was a step too far for any buffalo to be seen wearing such a garish necklace.

When they got home, Rekha got off the scooter and called Ram who came running as if his life depended on it.

"Ram, go with Sunny. Panditji says Daisy is in Ladowali Road. Bring her back quickly."

Ram looked surprised and exchanged glances with Sunny who shot him a warning look.

"But, Bibiji, how did Panditji know? How did…"

Rekha cut him short. "Stop asking questions and

bring her back before she moves on."

Ram climbed onto the back of the scooter and they rode off. When they got to Ladowali Road, they peered left and right but there was no sign of Daisy. Sunny rode along slowly thinking that his mother had lost all sanity. He began muttering to Ram about charlatans exploiting vulnerable women. Suddenly, Ram began shouting and pointing to a herd of buffalos that seemed to materialise at the side of the road.

There, on an empty plot of land, was a cluster of ten to fifteen buffalos grazing. Sunny stopped the scooter. Ram jumped off and ran towards the middle of the herd. There stood Daisy, chewing grass without a care in the world, with her cotton flowered collar around her neck. Ram had never been so happy to see a buffalo in his life! He threw his arms around her and rubbed her lovingly on her side.

Daisy looked up slowly and moved her head up and down as if nodding thoughtfully. Later, Ram would tell Rekha he thought Daisy was smiling when she saw him! Sunny got off the scooter and looked around. He could not see anybody with the herd. They probably ran off when they saw us coming, he thought, which was a shame as he was always ready for a fight.

"Ram, bring her home. I will go ahead and tell Ma

the good news. God knows how she got out here, miles from home, and how that *Pandit* knew she was here."

As he got back on the scooter and rode home, Sunny reflected on the day. India was a mystery to him. When they lived in the Midlands in England, there were no buffalos to worry about or astrologers who could tell you exactly where your buffalo had gone when it went missing.

Rekha was overjoyed when he told her that Daisy had been found on Ladowali Road. She enthused about Panditji and said the man was a saint. Sunny looked doubtful but he did not argue with his mother, as he could not explain how Panditji had known where Daisy was.

When Ram turned up with Daisy half an hour later, Rekha ran out and gave the buffalo a big hug.

"Where did you go to, Daisy?" she asked. "Fancied a jaunt, did you? We are going to have to watch over you like a hawk in the future." Daisy looked bored and made her way to her trough and within minutes she was chewing greens.

Sunny looked at his mother quizzingly. "Ma," he said, "how did Panditji know?"

Rekha looked at him with a smile. "This is India, Sunny. Land of saints and astrologers. They just know."

Pink Letters

I

"Letter for you," sang Ravi, bounding into the room waving a small square envelope.

"It's very pink," he said, handing it to his younger sister Neena, who was sitting on a rug on the floor, her brow furrowed as she read the book resting on her crossed knees.

She had reached a particularly gripping part. The plot had twisted unexpectedly and she resented the interruption.

"Huh? Who's it from?" she said, taking the envelope and looking at it suspiciously. It bore an Indian stamp bearing a photograph of Mahatma Gandhi.

She could not hide her disappointment that it wasn't from England. She looked forward to receiving letters from her old friends and teachers whom she still missed even after being away for a whole year.

The arrival of the letter puzzled her. It was the summer recess at her school in India and most of her friends lived nearby. They dropped in at each other's houses so there was no need to write. Her few friends who had gone up to the hill stations at Simla and Dalhousie to avoid the searing heat of the Punjab plains were not the writing sort.

She looked at the writing on the envelope, which was considerably neater than her own. The author had used a fountain pen and black ink. She was impressed, as she had not yet mastered the art of writing with a nib. When she tried, she smudged ink across the page.

The letter was definitely addressed to her. Turning it over for any clues about the sender, she found that the back of the envelope was blank.

"Well?" said Ravi, hovering nearby. "Aren't you going to open it?"

Neena was struck by Ravi's curiosity. If anything, he was more bored than she was by the long school recess. Despite the fact that he was five years older, they had become inseparable playmates since the family migrated the previous year.

At first, the move to India seemed like a big adventure. However, five months after they arrived, in December 1971, India and Pakistan went to war over East Pakistan. India supported East Pakistan's fight for independence in what became one of the shortest wars in history. After just thirteen days Pakistani troops surrendered and Bangladesh came into existence.

Nothing had prepared Ravi and Neena for the war and while it lasted their mother wailed daily at their father that they should never have left England.

In a funny kind of way it was exciting at first. The sound of sirens pierced the air, warning of enemy attack, and the schoolchildren ran out of the classrooms to gather in a field away from the buildings.

At home, a raid meant putting out all the lights and hiding in the windowless and airless internal hall until the all-clear sounded. The ground shuddered as bombs dropped nearby.

After a particularly frenzied bombing spree by the Pakistani air force, the Indian army shot down a Pakistani plane near their grandparents' village. Their father went to check that his in-laws were safe, which they were. He returned home with bits of the aircraft's tail carrying the Pakistani flag. When

Neena realised what a narrow escape her family had had, the war became a little less exciting and much more frightening.

Neena had been surprised and perturbed at the patriotic fervour that seized her classmates. She watched as her classmate Gita produced mini-posters with slogans like "Crush Pakistan "and "*Jai Hind*", which she discovered meant, "Long live India". Others sang popular Bollywood songs, changing the lyrics to abuse the leaders of Pakistan. Apparently, similar words were being used in Pakistan against Indians. She found this uncomfortable and incomprehensible.

In England, she had been unaware of any animosity between the two countries. Her parents had Pakistani friends and they spent time in each other's houses, sharing stories of the Punjab and eating the same food. Growing up in England, Neena had been subjected to racism. She knew what it was like to experience hate and she was depressed witnessing the hate generated by the war.

Quite apart from the war, Ravi and Neena had discovered that pretty much everything was different in India. It was a lot hotter and more chaotic, and nobody seemed to adhere to any rules. Queuing was unheard of and direct questioning about personal matters appeared the norm. The latter was frequently accompanied by a grin and a long inquisitive look.

Back in England, there was a park at the bottom of their street where Neena and Ravi used to hang out with their friends. There was nothing similar here so now, when Neena was bored, she would pester Ravi for books to read. Having nothing else to offer, he would hand over the novels he was reading for his English course at college and she would devour the densest books in days.

She was reading one of his books when Ravi bounded in waving the pink missive.

"Aren't you going to open it?" said Ravi plonking himself down in a chair.

Neena tore open the envelope and pulled out a sheet of pink paper.

"Someone really likes the colour pink,' said Ravi. "Is it from the Pink Panther?"

They laughed. Although Ravi could be annoying, Neena had to admit that he was often quite funny.

"So, who's it from and how much ransom are they demanding for the teddy bear?" said Ravi impishly. "Don't tell me. They want ten *samosas* and five *pakoras*."

Neena giggled as she turned the paper over. It was signed by somebody called "Satinder", but she didn't know anyone of that name.

It must be a mistake, she thought, but then again, it did begin with a salutation in her name.

She began to read but not out loud. She wanted to check what it said before blurting it out to Ravi.

Dear Neena,
I write to you on this paper pinky pink.

She glanced at Ravi and rolled her eyes.

"What is it, Neens?"

"I surmise it is from a nutter," she replied.

"Eh? What do you mean?"

"I mean it's from a nutcase. All that time you spent in a public school. Wasted!"

"Why do you say that it's from a nutcase?" Ravi replied. "And by the way, it's not nice to refer to someone as a nutcase."

She ignored him and read more.

You will be surprised to receive this. My name is Satinder. I am in eighth standard at St Mary's Convent School. My cousin, Kamal Sandhu, is your classmate. We cycle past you every day on our way to school.

Neena frowned. Kamal Sandhu was indeed a classmate of hers. But why would her cousin be writing to her? She and Kamal were in sixth standard so Kamal's cousin would be a few years older. Neena racked her brains. She recalled that on her rickshaw journey to school and back, Kamal often passed her on her bicycle. She always rang her bicycle bell manically and waved with one hand as she whizzed past. This would make Neena smile as she watched Kamal wobble precariously. Kamal was always accompanied by a plain-looking older girl who smiled as they both sailed by. Neena had not paid any attention to her until now. She realised that this was probably Kamal's cousin. The most annoying letter writer.

She read on.

I hope you don't mind me writing to you. Kamal often tells me stories about you. You sound very interesting. She says, when the teacher asked you to sing an English song to your class, you sang a funny song about hair-cutting that everybody liked. She also said you cannot speak Hindi and speak with a strange accent. I think she also said that you were very good at hockey. I love playing hockey.

Neena turned the page over.

> *Anyway, the reason for my writing is to ask if you would mind becoming my pen pal. My English needs improving and as I understand you have recently arrived from England, you could help me improve. Perhaps you could start by telling me what you have been doing over the summer holidays? My address is at the bottom of the letter if you care to write back.*
>
> *Best wishes*
> *Satinder*

Neena had been so engrossed in reading the letter that she had not noticed that Ravi had got up from the chair and come to stand behind her. He was reading the letter over her shoulder.

"How quaint!" he said. "Satinder wants to be your pen pal."

Neena felt angry. She was annoyed that Kamal had been talking about her and was embarrassed about the singing episode.

As if he had read her mind, Ravi asked, "What was the song you sang about hair cutting?"

"I can't remember," she lied. "I don't know any songs about hair cutting."

She remembered perfectly. It was a Monkees song she had memorised from the music magazine Ravi brought with him when they migrated to India. Her logic was that it was always good to know the words of at least one song in case you had to sing in public. It was a silly song that she had randomly come across and now she wished she had made a more suitable selection. She realised now that her classmates were not going to be impressed by a song with a refrain that asked, "Why don't you cut your hair?" Especially as many of them were Sikhs and one of the five things that a good Sikh must not do is cut their hair.

"Are you going to write back?" asked Ravi.

"No," said Neena sniffily. "I don't wish to encourage correspondence from people who don't know how to write a letter. I mean, since when do you put your address at the end?"

"I think you should, little Miss Pompous. Might be nice to have an Indian pen pal, and you could practise your Hindi."

Neena grunted and turned back to her book. "You do it if you're so interested," she said, flipping the letter to one side.

Ravi bent over and picked it up. He looked at it for a while and then put it back down beside his sister.

II

It took a few days, but Ravi managed to convince Neena to respond to Satinder's letter. They were sitting together on the sofa. Neena had a notebook, and gingerly held a fountain pen. She passed it from hand to hand, trying to decide whether to use her left or her right. In England she had always used her left hand, but here in India they had insisted on her writing with the right hand. The right hand, they said, was for eating and the left hand was for cleaning your posterior. To do otherwise was sinful and asking for trouble. Neena could not understand the logic and she found it all a bit confusing.

"Maybe we should do a draft first?" Ravi suggested.

"Maybe we shouldn't reply at all."

"C'mon Neens. It's fun! Where's your sense of adventure?"

"It died in the heatwave that's going to kill me too. Now, let's get this straight. If I do this, you will buy me a large mango *kulfi* when the ice-cream man comes around. Deal?"

Ravi grinned back at his sister. "When did you become so mercenary?"

"When I discovered you have a weakness for pink stationery! I think I'll tell her about the snake we found in the garage," she went on, "or the swarm of hornets that chased you and stung your face at the well in the village, or the…"

Ravi interrupted. "All good ideas, Neens, but maybe we need to keep it, kind of like, a bit less dramatic? Don't want her to think that we are accident prone, do we? What about beginning by saying what a pleasant surprise it was to receive her letter, and then tell her what you've been doing this summer. Like, you could say something about the book you're reading and the wedding we attended last week."

"Grrgh,' Neena groaned. "You have been giving it some thought, haven't you? I have a better idea. Why don't you draft it then I'll write it in my handwriting and sign it?"

"Not sure about that."

"Ravi, it's a great plan. And it's quicker. Go on, it will only take you five minutes."

Ravi considered the idea. His sister had outwitted him again. But what harm would it do?

"Okay, but on the condition you have to read what I have written and agree it's accurate."

"Agreed."

He quickly wrote a couple of paragraphs about the book Neena was reading and described the wedding they had attended. Then he asked what

Satinder had been doing and if she would like to visit.

Neena read over what Ravi had scribed.

"No. Not that bit about visiting," she said.

"Why not?"

"Because she is not my friend, Ravi. She's a pen friend, with an emphasis on 'pen'." She waved the fountain pen in front of him to illustrate her point.

Ravi sighed. He was about to say something when the shouts of the ice-cream seller could be heard coming from the street.

Excited, Neena looked at her brother.

"Ravi, you promised!"

"Okay, greedy guts," he said, getting up from the seat slowly. "I'll fetch us some while you write the letter."

As he reached the door, he turned around to check. Neena was writing carefully, biting her bottom lip in concentration as she tried not to smudge the page. He smiled to himself as he took some rupees from his back pocket and shut the door.

III

The reply arrived a week later. Again it came in a pink envelope. Neena ripped it open and pulled out a pink sheet of paper.

Ravi watched her with interest.

"Read it aloud," he said. Neena gave him a bored look.

Dear Neena,

Thank you for your letter. It was so nice hearing from you. It has been a long summer. I have spent some of it on vacation in Manali visiting my relatives. It was quite pleasant there. We went for some nice walks.

I am busy studying now. We have class examinations on my return to school. I am worried about the English and Maths exams as these are my weakest subjects. My father has organised extra tuition for me, which is helping.

What else have you been doing? Have you seen any new films? I look forward to hearing from you soon.

Best wishes,
Satinder

"That's it!" Neena exclaimed, throwing the letter down on the table in front of her.

"What do you mean?"

"What I mean, Ravi, is no more letters. I've had enough. This girl is so boring! Heaven knows why she has latched on to me, but I'm not writing back."

Ravi picked up the letter and studied it for a few minutes.

"Come on, Neens. It's not too much effort. I'll help you."

"I don't need your help!" Neena was getting seriously irritated with him. "I've no idea why you're so interested. *You* can write back if you're so bothered. And I am not taking bribes from you either. Ravi, this girl is demented. She tracks me down, plagues me with pink letters, and you seem to think this is all fine!"

"Okay, okay, keep your hair on!" Ravi gave his sister a resigned look and dropped the letter on the table. "Actually, I am not that bothered either. Do what you want."

"I will," said Neena defiantly. But she felt a flicker of guilt about snapping at Ravi. She knew he was just trying to fill the long empty days and, like her, was missing his old friends in England.

IV

True to her word, Neena did not write back, and no further letters arrived from Satinder. The summer recess came to an end. She went back to school and Ravi went to college. Neena's school had introduced a bus service for its pupils, so instead of getting a rickshaw she got the bus. Many of her friends did the same, and they saved a seat for her. On the first day back, she told them about the pink letters. They were as perplexed as she was but soon found other things to talk about and the incident was forgotten.

Kamal Sandhu did not mention the letters or her cousin either. She still cycled to school, but Neena no longer saw her pass every day as the school bus went a different route. Everybody was concentrating on the end of year exams which were due in two months.

The exams marked the end of the academic year. The weather got colder as winter approached. Neena anxiously awaited the results that would determine if she had made it to the seventh grade.

When she arrived in India, it took her a while to understand the assessment system. A failure in one subject would not prevent a student progressing to the next grade, which was good for Neena as she could not see herself passing the Hindi exams, having only just managed to learn the alphabet.

However, a failure in two subjects would be another story. This left the poor student with a choice. The first option was to repeat the whole year, which was humiliating as it meant that ex-classmates would be in the class above. The second option was to leave for another school where the student could join the class above as if they had not failed. The problem with this was that everybody would know. St Mary's Convent School for girls was the best school in the city. It was the only one to prepare its pupils to sit the prestigious Indian Certificate of Secondary Education.

Neena was delighted to discover she had passed all the exams except Hindi. Kamal Sandhu was not so fortunate and disappeared having failed three exams.

But pleasure at her school success was short-lived as things took an unfortunate turn at home. Ravi decided he wanted to return to England. He had found it difficult to adjust to the Indian curriculum and had become concerned about his chances of pursuing a career back in the UK if he stayed in India. Neena did not want him to go but she could see that he was unhappy. He promised to write. He promised not to use pinky pink paper and he encouraged her to continue reading books.

It was an emotional goodbye. Neena, who had argued with her older brother almost daily, found herself wishing he would change his mind. The day of his departure arrived and he walked her to the bus stop. His flight was leaving later that evening and their father was taking him to the airport. When her school bus arrived, they hugged awkwardly. Ravi patted Neena's head for good measure before he walked away without turning around.

Her friends were surprised to see her in tears when she sat down in her usual seat. She told them about Ravi and they consoled her.

"Such a shame – your brother is so handsome," said Shaminder gloomily.

This made Neena snort, and soon she was laughing at their jokes and stories. They could always cheer her up.

IV

Neena stared at her watch. The second hand was barely moving. She wondered if it had got stuck. She shook her wrist gently and put it to her ear before studying the watch face again.

"Go and wash your face in cold water," the teacher said in Hindi.

She looked up to see Mrs Malhotra, the Hindi teacher, staring down at her.

"Sorry. I don't understand," she replied.

"Tell her to go and wash her face in cold water," Mrs Malhotra said to Gita, the girl sitting in the chair next to Neena. "She has been staring forever at her watch."

Neena understood what was being said. Her Hindi was slowly improving. Obviously, Mrs Malhotra thought she could still not understand.

Gita nudged her friend gently with her knee. Neena understood it was wise not to annoy Mrs Malhotra. Watched by her classmates and feeling rather embarrassed, she got up from her seat and made her way out of the classroom. She did not want to have to go downstairs and walk along two corridors to the water tap, but Mrs Malhotra had made it clear, it was not a choice.

Splashing the cool water over her face, she was annoyed with herself for getting caught. She would have to be more careful not to show her boredom next time. Mrs Malhotra would be watching her like a hawk.

Slowly she made her way back to the classroom, hoping that Ramu, the school caretaker, would ring the bell indicating the end of the lesson. Again she looked at her watch. The cause of her embarrassment was telling her that the lesson still had ten minutes to go. She was shuffling along when she spied another girl in front of her. The girl turned around and they stared at each other for a few seconds. The girl's face registered recognition followed by a look of horror. Neena realised that it was Satinder, Kamal's cousin and the author of the pinky pink letters. She was going to say something to her but as she quickened her pace, Satinder did the same.

It was forbidden to run in the corridors and Neena was impressed with how fast Satinder managed to move without breaking into a run. She had longer legs and was making full use of them. Neena was shorter and she imagined she looked quite comical walking so fast, but she was not going to let the opportunity pass to have a conversation with the mysterious letter-writer. Taking a chance she ran up a side staircase to her left, and then ran past the library which had no windows, so afforded her some protection from being seen by a teacher. She circled around and reached the top of the main staircase, which she knew Satinder would be climbing.

Neena walked breathlessly down the steps. Satinder was coming up and because she was looking behind her got a surprise when she saw Neena blocking her way.

"Hello! Remember me?" said Neena.

"What do you want?" Satinder's eyes darted around nervously.

"I want to know why you wrote to me, Miss Pinky Pink."

Satinder looked flustered. "Oh that," she said. "I thought you might be an interesting pen pal and I wanted to practise my English. But, as I discovered, you are quite boring."

Neena could not believe her ears.

"What on earth are you talking about? Boring! How dare you?"

"My cousin, Kamal gave me the impression you were interesting. Anyway, it was a mistake."

Neena struggled to control her temper.

"Listen you. If it wasn't for my interfering brother, I wouldn't have written back at all. Blame him for the boring bits. He wrote them!"

Shocked, Satinder exclaimed, "Your brother! You let your brother write to me!"

"Well, no. I wrote the letter but he drafted it."

Satinder looked horrified. She leaned in and whispered menacingly, "Listen to me. You better not repeat that to anyone else or you will be sorry. In India, boys don't write to girls unless they are scoundrels."

"My brother may be many things but he is not a scoundrel," said Neena angrily. "The hypocrisy of this country is incredible. You can't have male friends, but you watch films in which boys pester girls and fall in love and nobody questions that. You ought to be grateful that my brother is boring. If he was anything like your film heroes, he would be married to you by now!"

There was a pause for a few seconds whilst Satinder absorbed Neena's words.

"Look" said Satinder adopting a more affable tone "I am sorry. It was a bad idea, but actually it was not even my idea."

Neena looked at her puzzled "What do you mean? Whose idea was it?"

"My tutor, Mrs Sharma. To help me improve my English, my father arranged tuition for me during the holidays. Mrs Sharma suggested it. She said it might help my English if I conversed with somebody for practice. When she asked me if I knew somebody who was fluent in English, I thought of you. She helped me draft the letters."

"Surely, she didn't tell you to add the pinky pink bit? What kind of an English tutor is she?" Neena exclaimed.

"No. That was my idea" said Satinder sheepishly. "When Mrs Sharma saw my letter, she told me to take it out, but I forgot. Anyway, at the time, I thought it was a quaint English expression."

Neena started to laugh. She tried to stop but found it difficult.

"What is so funny?" asked Satinder.

"You could not make it up! Mrs Sharma thought she was helping you improve your English by writing to me, but she was actually corresponding with my sixteen-year-old brother. A married woman writing to a boy, Indian society would be appalled!"

Satinder started to laugh too. "Ha! Ha! That is funny! It would make a good story for a Hindi film."

They both laughed. Then Neena realised that Mrs Malhotra would be wondering where she had got to.

"I had better go otherwise Mrs Malhotra will be pulling my ears. She already thinks that I am an idiot."

Satinder gave her a quizzical look.

"Long story. Anyway, next time you want to practise your English, just speak to me, okay? You may discover that I am not so boring after all."

Satinder nodded as they climbed the stairs. At the top they said "Bye" to each other, and Neena watched as Satinder walked down the corridor in the opposite direction to her own classroom. She looked at her watch again. Three minutes left. Then she had a thought.

She looked at the school bell hanging invitingly in front of her. A quick look around indicated that nobody was in sight. Neena reached forward and grabbed the rope which made the bell ring. She gave it three strong tugs. Its ring echoed down the corridors. She quickly walked towards her classroom.

By the time, she reached the door, Mrs Malhotra was packing up her books and handbag. She walked briskly past Neena saying, "Next time, pay attention, child. Hindi is a beautiful language worth learning. Your parents ought to have taught you to speak our mother tongue." She tutted loudly.

Neena nodded without meeting her teacher's gaze. She walked into the classroom to be greeted with laughter from her friends who imitated her looking at her watch and snoring loudly.

I Will Send You Love Songs

I

She stood on the stage before me, dressed in an electric blue *sari* studded with sequins that twinkled as they caught the sun when she moved her body in time with the music. Her raven hair was piled high and swept back, circling her head like a halo. She had wide, brown eyes and bright red lipstick, reminding me of Miss India from the Miss World contest I had watched on television.

Later, when I reflected on the day, I realised it was the song that seduced me. She was merely the medium through which it reached my whole being.

In her sultry voice, she introduced it as the song of lovers. It began with a thumping blast from a *dhol* drum, which made my whole body shake and my heart feel as though it was trying to burst free from my chest. When she began to sing the words, I was lost.

It was my cousin Vijay's wedding. He sat beaming, enjoying all the attention piled upon him. Handsome in his crisp new navy suit, he tapped his foot in rhythm with the beat and clapped his hands. I sat next to him, my eyes wide with amazement and my mouth open with surprise. It may have been his wedding, but it was my song.

I was twelve years old. My family had recently migrated to India from the UK and this was the first Punjabi wedding I had ever attended. Prior to this, I had no idea how much Punjabis loved bright colours, dancing and singing. My feet were sore from the previous day's marathon, when everyone was expected to join the energetic steps of the Punjabi's favourite dance, the *Bhangra*.

The words of the song echoed in my head for days. Roughly translated, they were, "I am going to take a lover, I don't care what people might say. Nothing is going to put me off. Even if people spread malicious rumours." I found myself humming the tune over and over again.

I discovered it was a traditional folk song from the Punjab that was adapted for a Bollywood film and the songstress was a well-known Punjabi folk singer. She sang about a dozen songs that day at Vijay's wedding, but I could only ever remember one, "The Love Song".

II

Anita was my best friend. I had told my mother that I was going to her house to study and do homework. I lied. Neither of us had any intention of doing either. Within five minutes of arriving at Anita's she suggested, with the sly sideways look she gave me when she had pre-planned something adventurous, that we visit the market. She was a mischievous girl like me which is why we got on so well. I didn't need much persuading. Her promise of a plateful of *samosas* when we got there sealed the deal.

Conveniently, Anita's parents were out. We decided to take my bike. As I began cycling down the road, Anita jumped on the back, expertly landing on the metal rear rack. The bike wobbled but I managed to control the handlebars and off we went. Before long we reached the bustling market, which was alive with the sound of Bollywood songs being played through loudspeakers. The smell of frying *samosas* and curries filled my nostrils.

A rainbow of *saris*, hanging precariously on horizontal poles, adorned the exterior of shops. Fruit stalls laden down with luscious mangoes, golden guavas and huge watermelons stood side by side, emitting tantalising tropical smells and adding a riot of colour to the scene. The market hawkers called out to passers-by, "Hot *pakoras*, hot *samosas*. Get them here" and "New fashion suits. Japanese print *saris*. Come inside and see!"

We dismounted from the bike and I wheeled it along. It wasn't long before the comments started. "Hello baby doll! I love you" and "Such beauties! God kill me now!" or a stray hand would rub against our backs or legs. Leering teenage boys and dirty-looking men stared at us. Our footsteps quickened in response.

I was becoming anxious at the unwanted attention we were attracting but Anita glared at them whilst firing comments back: "Get lost, bastard" and "Have you no sisters, shameless donkey?" I was surprised to learn that a twelve-year-old knew so many swear words. Feeling exposed, I pulled my *kurta* away from me in the hope it would make my body appear more androgynous.

I was beginning to think that visiting the market had been a very bad idea. As if she had read my mind, Anita turned and looked at me. "Ignore them," she hissed. "These useless layabouts have nothing else to do. Come on, let's get some hot *samosas*."

As we increased our pace, I noticed a man on my right standing next to a stall selling postcard photographs of Bollywood stars and magazines. There was a poster at the front which said "*Filmfare* and *Stardust* here. Buy posters, photos and songs." Suddenly a thought struck me and I grabbed Anita's arm, making her jump and almost dropping the bike as I did so. "Wait, Anita! Let's take a look." She stopped and we walked over to the stall. "Great!" she exclaimed, "I want the words of the film *Pakeezah* which has just been released."

As we sifted through the song sheets on display, I racked my brains to think of the title of the film my love song was from. Then, suddenly, it came to me! I asked the stall holder if he had the film. He looked through a box under the table and pulled out the sheet. "Ten paisa only," he said with a toothy grin. I quickly looked through the tatty sheet. I was over the moon. I handed over the money and soon had the barely decipherable copy in my hands.

It was getting late so I decided I ought to

be heading home. Anita looked disappointed, particularly as we had not had any *samosas*, but after making me promise we would visit the market again, I cycled back to her house to drop her off.

As we said our farewells, Anita showed me the copy of the *Filmfare* magazine she had purchased at the market. "Look," she pointed at the cover "It's Rajesh Khanna. Wow! He looks so handsome. Did you know women write him letters using their own blood?"

"Ugh! That's disgusting!"

Anita pulled a face. "I wouldn't go to such trouble. Far simpler to use red ink. Same effect."

We both laughed. This is what I loved about Anita. She was a minx. I cycled home with the lyrics of my song safely in my pocket and a smile on my face.

III

The sun was merciless. The bike ride home from school in the sweltering heat left me feeling hot and bothered. Amrit, my younger sister, refused to cycle and insisted on sitting on the back of the bike. So I did all the work, sweating profusely with the weight of pedalling two people and a couple of heavy school bags.

We often argued about the fact she never took a turn at pedalling. Frequently, she tried flattery. "It's just that you are a much better cyclist than me," or "you have stronger legs than me" or "It's your bike. I don't want to damage it."

Despite my reassurances that she too could be a great cyclist if she cycled more, and she also could have strong legs if she experienced the fun of cycling with two people and their full bags, and yes, theoretically it was my bike however I had a sharing nature so I was happy to have her use it. But it all fell on deaf ears.

Arriving home, we ran inside to get under the cooling ceiling fan. Mum was in the main bedroom sitting on a chair. As I ran in and flung myself onto the bed, she looked disapprovingly at me. The *chappal* on her right foot was tapping on the floor which was a very bad sign.

"Hi Mum, what's for lunch?" Amrit piped in. "I need a glass of water. It's so hot out there."

I shot her a look of annoyance, wondering why she was so thirsty when I had been the one doing all the hard work.

Mum looked straight at me "So, who are you sending letters to?"

"What?" I said, raising my eyebrows.

"I was tidying your room this morning and I found this," she said, producing the lyrics of the song I had purchased at the market.

Because the sheet was so filthy and was falling apart, I had painstakingly written out the lyrics on a clean sheet of paper and discarded the original. This was my first mistake. My second was to title it, "The Love Song" and draw red hearts entwined all down the sides.

"Oh, that," I said, "they are just the words of the song I liked."

Mum jumped off the chair. Taking her *chappal* off her foot, she hit me with it sharply on my leg.

"Ow! Ow! What's that for?" I cried out in pain.

"I will send you love songs," she shouted. "Here, shameless girl, here is a love song for you." She threw her other *chappal* at me as I ran out the room.

"It is only a song," I protested from the safety of the doorway.

"That's how it all starts," shouted Mum. "First love songs, then love letters, then love meetings, then God knows what."

"Then wedding bells," murmured Amrit mischievously. I glared at her.

"It could've been Amrit. Why do you always think it was me?"

"A mother knows her children," she replied. "Like the time you hid the packet of cigarettes in the drawer with the old rags for cleaning. Remember? I knew it was you."

"Was it the nicotine on my fingers or my tobacco stained teeth?" I retorted under my breath.

"Don't be cheeky! Don't let me catch you doing anything like this again!"

"I'm sorry. I just liked the song. It moved me."

"I will move you into the shed if you keep this up. Enough now. Come to the kitchen. The food is ready."

Amrit and I followed her into the kitchen where she switched on the radio, which was tuned into All India Radio, playing Bollywood songs. Mum had her back to us as we sat at the table.

"I am going to take a lover. I don't care what people might say," the words wafted melodiously out of the speakers.

Amrit looked at me as she silently mouthed the words, jiggling her head suggestively, and fluttering her eyelashes.

I rolled my eyes and drank a glass of water.

CHICKEN CURRY

"Look out! Papa is coming down the lane and he doesn't look too happy." Madhu, my younger sister, ran into our yard breathless.

I got up from the chair I was sitting on, closed the book I was reading, and put on my *chappals*. Then I ran towards the house.

My older sister, Sukhi, who was sitting on the string bed in front of me painting her toenails, swung her feet over the side and jumped off. She too ran towards the house.

Madhu warned Ma who was in the kitchen cooking.

Papa opened the front door, which was made of heavy steel.

Sukhi and I peered at him through the bamboo blinds which ran along the front verandah of the house. Madhu was right. He did not look happy.

Papa walked in angrily and quickly closed the door after him. He had barely bolted it before he yelled out, "Sukhi, Prakash, Madhu, where are you? Come here immediately!"

Sukhi and I exchanged glances nervously. "Go and see what he wants," she whispered.

"No way!" I whispered back. "Anyway, you first."

"Oy, I can see you looking through the blinds," he roared. "Come out now."

Madhu and Ma emerged from the kitchen. Sukhi and I sheepishly lifted the bamboo blind and walked out into the yard.

"Why the shouting?" Ma asked. "Do you want the whole village knowing our business? What is it that is so bad that you have taken to bellowing at the girls?"

Papa glared at her and pointed at the three of us. We stood with our eyes downcast, wracking our brains, trying to work out which of our most recent misdemeanours had come to light.

"Thanks to these three, the whole village is talking about us."

"Really?" Ma replied. "What do you mean?"

He wiped his sweating brow with the cloth he sometimes wore around his neck.

"I was at the Diwan Gate. Balbir Singh told me that Sant Singh had been there earlier, complaining about the girls making too much noise. He said that they were always arguing and fighting amongst themselves and it kept him awake."

The Diwan Gate was the gateway to the village. It was a building with an archway where the elderly men of the village often idled away the hours sitting and gossiping. Although Papa was not elderly, he loved to get his fix of juicy gossip then return home to convey the best bits to Ma.

Ma would listen to him, but she did not approve of this activity. She was often scathing about the men who sat there, describing them as dirty old men whose real motive was to perv at the village women as they walked past and discuss them once they thought they were out of earshot.

Ma looked at us then back at Papa.

"What exactly did Sant Singh say?" she asked.

"He said that our daughters were always fighting with each other. They are noisy and misbehaved with no shame. They shout and keep him awake when he tries to take his siesta at the back of his farm building. What have you three got to say for yourselves? I have never been so embarrassed in my life! I had to leave and come home."

I felt like saying, "Sant Singh is a fine one to talk with his filthy swearing and shouting," but I thought it best to keep quiet. Last time I answered back, Papa made me do eight hundred pumps at the hand pump. My arms started to throb painfully at the memory. Papa used to be in a military academy, then the police force. The experiences had bequeathed him an endless supply of punishments.

Sant Singh was a grumpy, unsmiling man who always wore a grubby white turban and a dirty *kurta* and *chador*. He lived next door with his wife Jageero, son Tari, and daughter-in-law Rano. Like many in the village he was a farmer, and his farm backed up to the rear of the house. Our windows looked out onto his farmstead. Sant Singh was often seen feeding his buffalos or watering his crops. He would sometimes take a nap on a string bed in the shade of a mango tree.

Not long before, looking out of the window, I had seen him behaving suspiciously. He was carrying clay pots and building a contraption with a fire beneath it. So absorbed was he that he did not notice me watching him.

I beckoned Sukhi and Madhu over to the window.

"What's he up to?" I whispered.

"I think he is making *sharaab*, alcohol," said Sukhi.

For a few minutes we watched him silently, until Madhu piped up.

"Do you think he is going to boil his clothes? I don't think they would survive a wash!"

This set us off. We tried to stifle our laughter but the more we tried, the harder it got, until snorts emerged from our covered mouths.

Sant Singh looked up. Afraid he had seen us, we ducked.

That was a couple of weeks ago. Now Papa was looking directly at us. His eyes were wide with fury and his nostrils flared like a horse about to stampede. None of us wanted to meet his gaze.

"Fine. If you are going to behave like donkeys then you will be treated like donkeys. Follow me."

He marched us across the yard to the poultry building which adjoined the house. He owned the poultry farm, which was divided into four sections. In two of the sections, the chickens roamed freely. The third section was for chicks when there were any, and the fourth section stored equipment. The sections were separated by walls and connecting doors, which were kept closed. The whole building was made of brick and had large wire mesh windows which allowed fresh air to circulate. From inside the building, you could look out and survey the surrounding fields and farms.

Papa opened the door to the equipment section. My heart sank.

"In there," he ordered.

We exchanged worried looks and Madhu started whimpering.

"None of that!" Papa barked. "You are not the daughters of a Nawab."

I tried to see Ma's reaction but, with Papa in the way, I could not. We trudged slowly into the room. Papa beckoned Roshan, the farmhand who helped on the poultry farm.

"Roshan, put the string bed in there."

Roshan looked at us, then at Papa. Having witnessed Papa's anger on numerous occasions, he was not going to argue, though I could tell he did not approve of this punishment. He lifted a bed and placed in the room.

"Now, shameless girls, argue to your heart's content," said Papa as he locked the door after us.

Turning to Ma, he said, "And don't you let them out of there until I say so." They disappeared into the kitchen and we could not see or hear them anymore.

We sat on the string bed for a few minutes,

absorbing what had just happened.

"Sant Singh is a bastard," declared Sukhi.

"Yes," I agreed. "He was angry because we caught him making booze."

"If you two hadn't started laughing and snorting, he wouldn't have heard us and he wouldn't have got annoyed," said Madhu, sniffling.

"Really? And remind me again, why we were laughing in the first place?" I asked, staring at her.

"Because you are an idiot," said Madhu.

"Or is it because you are a donkey?" said Sukhi.

"At least I don't bay like a donkey!" retorted Madhu.

"Better to bay like a donkey than snort like a pig!" I fired at Madhu.

"We are in here because you two are constantly arguing," said Sukhi, without an ounce of irony. We both looked at her in disbelief.

"What are you talking about? You are hardly Mother Theresa!" I said.

"Shut up," said Sukhi, "or I will wallop you."

"Just you just try it," I replied, rolling up the sleeves of my *kurta*.

"And my toe nails got ruined," Sukhi added.

"You are lucky Papa didn't catch you painting them," said Madhu.

"Stop it!" I said. "Unless you would rather be in with the chickens? If Papa hears us arguing, be sure we will end up in there with them."

"She's right," said Madhu. "Ceasefire?"

"Ceasefire," said Sukhi. "God, it's hot in here. Do you think we should ask Papa to get it air-conditioned?"

We laughed. The sun streamed in. It was around one o'clock in the afternoon, siesta time. We lay down on the bed. Outside it was quiet, apart from an occasional squawk from the chickens. Soon we were fast asleep.

About four o'clock, Ma opened the door. She came in and shook each of us gently.

"Get up," she said.

We awoke slowly. For a few minutes, I could not remember where we were. Then I saw the surroundings and remembered.

"Come on," said Ma, "I have put some food out in the kitchen."

Slowly we got up, looking at her suspiciously.

"Where is Papa?" asked Sukhi nervously.

"He's gone to the farm," Ma replied. "He won't be back for a few hours."

We followed her into the kitchen, where she had set up three plates of food and glasses of water.

We ate silently, shooting Ma glances every so often. She seemed lost in thought.

When we had finished, she removed the plates and washed them.

"Go and wash your faces. You look like cats have licked them," she said.

We went to the bathroom and splashed our faces with cold water.

Ma put her *dupatta* around her neck and head.

"Where are you going?" I said.

"Out," she replied.

"Can I come?" I asked.

She nodded. Madhu piped up. "I want to come too."

Ma nodded again.

Sukhi said, "I will stay here. I've got a maths test tomorrow and I don't want to fail because I have been locked in a chicken shed all afternoon." She fired Ma an angry look.

Ma looked back at her. "You study," she said.

Ma opened the door and Madhu and I ran to join her.

She walked quickly down the lane.

"Where is she going?" Madhu asked.

"No idea," I replied, shutting the door behind me.

Soon it became obvious. Ma stopped in front of

Sant Singh's house and banged her fist on the door.

After a minute Sant Singh's wife Jageero appeared.

"Welcome, welcome," she said on seeing us. "Come in. What an auspicious day it is that you are blessing us with a visit."

"*Sat Sri Akal*," said Ma, "have you got a minute?"

Jageero looked surprised. Ma did not visit many houses in the village, preferring instead to chat to people when she saw them in the lanes or on the way to the farm.

"Something happened?" asked Jageero, leading us into the kitchen where her daughter-in-law, Rano, sat chopping vegetables. Rano and Ma exchanged pleasantries.

"Is your husband home?" Ma asked Jageero.

"No," said Jageero, "he is out with the plough."

"Good," replied Ma. "Then you can convey a message to him."

Madhu and I watched Ma with surprise.

Suddenly, Ma grabbed a long knife from the table.

Shocked, Jageero and Rano stepped backwards. Ma turned and grabbed at Madhu and me with her free hand.

She waved the knife above her head and shouted, "Your husband is a troublemaker! He went to the

Diwan Gate and told everybody that my daughters are always fighting and arguing. Consequently their father locked them in the chicken shed for the whole afternoon to punish them."

Ma has gone mad, I thought.

Jageero and Rano looked at Ma open-mouthed.

"Why would he say such things? I am so sorry. I had no idea," Jageero spluttered.

"You know what their father is like," Ma went on. "He has a temper. My girls are good girls. They are full of energy and life. Yet your husband wants to put them in *purdah*! Seen and not heard. Well, here take this knife, Jageero, for I would rather you kill them now than they live lives empty of joy."

Jageero pleaded for Ma to give her the knife.

"If not them,' said Ma, "then kill *me* because I cannot watch this travesty."

I was shocked. This was like a Bollywood film being acted out in front of my eyes. Ma was Meena Kumari, the beautiful tragic actress.

By now, both Jageero and Rano were wailing and trying to throw themselves at Ma's feet. Ma tried to avoid this happening by dancing around the room.

Madhu and I watched, stunned.

"My husband is a fool," Jageero wept. "I will see to him when he gets home. He will never speak badly about your girls again. I promise you that, I swear."

Ma had made her point. Calmly, she put the knife down.

"That's all I ask for," she said. "My husband and his temper I will deal with, but you keep your word about yours."

Jageero nodded and wiped her eyes with the corner of her *dupatta*. She reached forward and grabbed Madhu and me and hugged us to her ample breast.

"They are like my own daughters," she said, as I fought against the smell of onions and sweat emanating from her clothes. I could see Madhu doing the same.

Ma signalled that we were leaving. She walked purposefully to the door and we followed.

When we were back in the lane, walking home, she turned to Madhu and me and said, "I think I will make chicken curry tonight. Would you like that?"

MONKEY BUSINESS

I

Kiran eyed him nervously. He sat on the window ledge looking down on her while chomping on the banana he held in his unkempt, hairy hands.

She did not want to venture any closer. She had watched him descend and ascend the pole to which he was secured at least a hundred times a day since he had arrived. She knew how quickly he could move. He sat observing her with disdain, which made her feel uncomfortable. She turned her face away and he seized the opportunity to throw the banana skin at her, whacking her smartly on the side of her head.

"Ow!" Kiran looked up with surprise. He grinned back, baring his teeth. Was he laughing at her? She couldn't tell for sure. He began making a growling noise, so she wasn't going to take any chances. They stared at each other for a while.

Just then, with a rusty creak, the gate swung open. Kiran looked over to see who it was. Her father, Dev, wheeled his bicycle in to the yard. He had been to the bazaar in the nearby town and the bicycle's handlebars were laden with cotton bags of fruit and vegetables.

Kiran could see that he was hot and bothered and sweating profusely. She jumped up and ran over to help him with the bags. He handed them to her and she carried them into the kitchen. Dev leaned the bicycle against the wall of the yard and followed her in.

"How's he been?" he asked whilst mopping his brow with the patterned cotton scarf he wore around his neck and shoulders.

"He hit me on the head with a banana skin."

Dev laughed. "So he has a good aim!"

Kiran glanced anxiously at her father. "Dad, he's aggressive. I'm frightened of him."

"Don't be," Dev replied as he emptied the vegetables from the bag into a basket. "He's just getting used to us. I'm sure he'll be fine in a couple of days."

Kiran looked unconvinced. She went over to the clay pot filled with cool water, poured Dev a glassful and handed it to him. He drank it in one gulp.

"More?" she asked.

He nodded.

As he wiped his forehead with the scarf, she poured him another glass.

Dev drank again. "Has he had some water?" He nodded his head in the direction of the monkey.

"Yes. Puran put some out for him earlier." Puran and Shankar were the two farmhands employed by Dev. They lived in accommodation on the adjacent side of the yard.

"Has he come down from the ledge?"

"Yes, he did, but I ran inside."

Dev grinned.

"He won't bite you," he said, rubbing his chin thoughtfully. "We need to give him a name."

"Let's ask Mum. After all, this was her idea."

Dev looked at Kiran crossly.

"Don't be disrespectful," he said with an edge to his voice. "Your mother is only thinking of ways to reduce your boredom."

Kiran stared back at him, puzzled.

"Reduce my boredom?"

"Yes. Your mother had a pet monkey when she was a child. Your grandfather got it from a contact when he was posted to Dharmkot. Because he was constantly being moved between locations, your mother was in and out of different schools and sometimes she got lonely. Having a monkey taught her a lot, especially about responsibility and caring about others. She had to ensure the monkey was fed and looked after. It proved educational."

Since their move to India three years ago, Kiran had realised that her parents were different to the other Indians around them. They were adventurous and took risks. This had its advantages as well as disadvantages. The advantages included a long list of family adventures, some of which she had enjoyed, but the occasional downside was an ill-thought-out and rash decision which led to arguments. She had a feeling the monkey business might be one of these.

Furthermore, she reflected, if they genuinely wanted to reduce her boredom, they could have asked for her ideas on the matter. She would have gladly suggested that they purchase a scooter for her to go out and visit her friends. Instead what did she get to reduce her boredom? A bad-tempered monkey.

Kiran kept these thoughts to herself, as she knew her father did not welcome positive criticism, especially when he was hot and bothered and just back from the bazaar.

She looked towards the courtyard with resentment. The monkey was getting far too much attention. He lacked manners and was insolent.

"Let's call him Shetan," she suggested mischievously.

"I don't think calling him the devil is such a good idea," Dev replied irritably. "What about Shero?"

Kiran rolled her eyes. "Isn't it a bit odd to call a monkey 'lion'? People may get the wrong idea and think we England-returned *desis* don't know the difference."

Dev threw her an odd look. Sometimes he could not tell if his daughter was being cheeky. This time, he decided to give her the benefit of the doubt. "I don't think people would think that. Many people in India name their dogs Shero. Vikram Choudary, the contractor, for example, has a Doberman called Shero." Dev paused while he finished downing the second glass of water. "Where's your mother, anyway?"

"Having a rest. She asked me to wake her later."

"Okay. Look, try and talk to him," Dev said after a minute. "It might help in getting over your fear."

No way, she thought.

Her father placed the empty glass on the table, put some peanuts from the jar on the shelf in his *kurta* pocket and went out into the yard.

"Shero! Shero!" he called.

Kiran watched from the kitchen door as the monkey now called Shero remained on the ledge, looking around without a care in the world.

"Shero *yaar*, my friend. Come down."

Dev tried to coax him down by taking some peanuts out of his pocket. Shero watched Dev inquisitively. Dev smiled and showed him what he held in the palm of his hand.

Shero slowly made his way down from the ledge. When he got to the bottom of the pole, he grabbed the nuts out of Dev's hand and stuffed them greedily into his mouth. He then scampered back up the pole and sat on the ledge.

Dev laughed but Kiran didn't join in.

Later, she watched Shero from the safety of the kitchen window. He was running up and down the pole, tormenting Jack. Jack was a fluffy bundle of black and tan fur that the family had acquired as a puppy from the Kangra valley soon after their arrival in India. Shero teased him mercilessly, pulling his tail and jumping on his back. Jack's normally placid nature was tested to the limit. He growled and barked, then avoided getting anywhere within reach of Shero.

II

It was true that Kiran suffered from boredom. Since her parents had taken the decision a year ago to move from the comfortable home they had built in the city to a small village in the Punjabi countryside, her life had once again been turned upside down. The friends she had made in the city were now over an hour's drive away. Although she was still attending her city school, the daily commute was leaving her exhausted. She had never become accustomed to her parents' need to move frequently.

In the mid-1950s, her parents had left the green and fertile plains of the Punjab in India for the industrialised post-war streets of the English Midlands. When the violent racism of the skinheads in the early 1970s began to impact upon their daily lives, they decided enough was enough. They sold everything they had and moved back to India.

Kiran had been born in England. Her older brothers Randeep and Jasvir had been born in India. When her parents returned to India, her brothers had opted to stay in England to attend university, but Kiran was only eleven years old and was not given a choice. Reluctantly, she had accompanied her parents.

However, her parents discovered that India had changed dramatically during their fourteen years absence. They found it difficult to adjust. At first, they thought that city living in India would suit them, but the snobbery and prejudices of their Indian neighbours appalled them. In a desperate attempt to regain the life they had lost in the years of working in low-paid manual jobs in Britain, her parents decided to move back to the village they had left. Sadly, they soon discovered that things had changed there too.

Living as immigrants in England had given them first-hand experience of unfair treatment and discrimination. Hence, the handsome and comfortably off young couple who had left for Britain with high hopes for a better future had returned to India educated in all aspects of inequality.

Britain had changed them. They discovered that their Indian qualifications held little value in post-war, ex-Raj Britain, so their job opportunities were limited. Their colour and ethnicity made them targets for racism. On their return, Indian norms like the caste system were anathema to them and their openly voiced abhorrence of any form of inequality made others view them with suspicion.

They were also unusual in that they had been the only members of their family to migrate. This meant that they had not had family support in England. Kiran's mother, Jassi, had frequently commented that nobody else in their family had emigrated because they had no need to, but she and Dev had wanted more.

Their Indian counterparts could not understand why these England-returned *desis* were so different to others who returned gloating about their wealth and wearing gaudy, sparkling clothes and jewellery and speaking "Punjlish" – a mixture of Punjabi and English merged together.

When Kiran questioned her mother about why other returning Indians were so different to them, Jassi told her that when she and Dev had first gone to England in the fifties, not many Indians were migrating. Of those that did, most were men. The women were left behind, and it was a decade or so later before men began to send for their wives and children. Jassi was the exception. She laughed when she told Kiran that, at first, she was very homesick and would chase any woman she saw dressed in a *salwar kameez*, begging them to come for tea. Dev had warned her against this practice, explaining that this kind of behaviour got people locked up in England.

On occasions, Kiran overheard her parents discuss visiting other *desis*.

"I saw that Nirmala from Slough walking past the *gurdwara* this morning," Jassi said to Dev during lunch one day. "She was tottering on heels that were two inches high and dressed like a Christmas tree in a fluorescent pink *salwar kameez* made of nylon. It's a wonder that the village dogs didn't attack her."

"How do you know it was made of nylon?" Dev asked incredulously.

"She was charged like an electric pylon and sparks of lightning were coming out of her hair!" Jassi enjoyed telling the tale. "And years of working as a seamstress in England have taught me to tell the difference between cotton, silk and nylon."

Dev grinned as Jassi continued, "Anyway, I don't know why she doesn't wear cotton. It's much more comfortable and you sweat less in this heat."

"Listen to you! You sound like a fashion writer for some *gora* magazine," Dev laughed.

"Laugh away. But if you had to wear nylon in this heat you would not find it so hilarious."

"True, but then I have the good fortune to have a

wife who is an expert on fabrics." Adopting a sadder tone, he added, "Anyway, all that Indians see is the wealth of the returnees. They don't necessarily see what sacrifices have been made to obtain that wealth."

III

After a few days, only Dev was prepared to engage with Shero. Everybody else, including Jassi, Puran and Shankar admitted they were frightened of him.

Dev was adamant that Shero would calm down and, in a day or two, be released from the leash attaching him to the pole. Jassi disagreed and an argument ensued.

"It will be fine," Dev said. "He just needs time to settle down."

"He isn't going to settle down. He is a wild thing and he growls. Everybody is scared of him. If you let him off his lead, he will wreak havoc."

"Listen. You had a monkey once. I am sure he wasn't domesticated when you first got him."

"He was a smaller monkey, not a baboon, and my father got him from a trusted friend."

"What are you saying?' Dev shouted. "Are you suggesting I brought a wild baboon into the house?"

"Yes, I am saying that! You asked the *bazigaar* for

a monkey and he got you a wild one. He is a traveller after all. I am not blaming him. I am blaming you!" She flashed her dark eyes.

Dev tried to control his temper. "It was your idea in the first place. God knows why I listen to you."

Jassi wasn't going to let him get away with that.

"Oh, I knew this would be my fault," she said. "Be very careful what you say next."

Dev muttered under his breath but knew better than to say more. The last time they had an argument, she refused to cook for him for two days. He did not want a repeat of that.

He decided to try another tack.

"Oh, I am not blaming or shaming. Just try to understand what I am saying, Baba. Leave it to me. I will deal with Shero. No need to get stressed."

"Fine," she retorted. "But I warn you now. Any trouble from that baboon and he goes back to the foothills of the Himalayas."

Shero was the most stubborn monkey ever. He seemed incapable of changing his behaviour. A week passed but he only came down the pole to tease the dog, scare anybody who dared to engage with him, and grab food. From his perch on the window, he pelted people with banana skins and anything else he got his hands on.

One day, Jassi put a basket of mangoes on the roof to ripen. Shero managed to lie flat and stretch his legs and feet so that the basket was in his grasp. He knocked the pile of fruit over and grabbed a few mangoes which he ate greedily. Then, much to Jassi's annoyance, he threw the hard seeds all over the yard.

Flies and ants descended. Jassi threw buckets of water over them and Puran helped clear up the mess.

Kiran heard her parents argue about the incident later.

The next day, she watched as Dev tried to coax Shero off the ledge with a banana. At first, Shero looked down at him with disdain. He even yawned a few times and stretched his arms before scratching his armpits. Fleas, no doubt thought Kiran. Shero needed a good bath but nobody was going to volunteer to give him one.

After five minutes of Dev's pleading, Shero came down the pole. Kiran was surprised as he meekly took the banana from Dev's outstretched hand. He sat there and peeled it before putting the skin on the ground beside him and stuffing the rest into his mouth.

Dev looked around gleefully.

"See! See!" he exclaimed. "Shero is a good monkey. He is learning. I told everybody he would."

As he said this, Shero leaned forward and grabbed Dev's hand. He sunk his teeth into the flesh, drawing blood, before running back up the pole.

"Argh!" Dev bellowed. "He bit me! The swine bit me! Quick, Kiran, send Puran to get the doctor!"

Kiran was already running towards Puran and shouting at him to fetch the doctor.

Jassi rushed out of the kitchen where she had been preparing lunch. She took one look at the teeth marks on her husband's bloody hand and realised what had happened.

"He bit you, didn't he? Right, that's it. He is going back now."

She ran into the house and returned with antiseptic and a clean towel.

"I have asked Puran to fetch the doctor," said Kiran.

Dev was still shouting obscenities.

"Where is Shankar? Tell him to go and get the *bazigaar*, Sohan, and tell him to bring a cage with him."

Shankar had heard the commotion from the chicken shed and came running. Nodding towards Dev, he grabbed a bicycle and rode out of the yard.

"Shankar, ensure Sohan knows this is urgent."

Kiran looked up to see what Shero was doing. He was sitting on the ledge grinning down at them.

IV

Dr Sharma gave Dev a tetanus injection and carefully cleaned the wounded hand before bandaging it.

"Sardarji," he said addressing Dev, "I am not sure it's a good idea keeping a wild monkey as a pet. There is a risk of all kinds of disease, not to mention the violence that this hairy chap is clearly capable of."

Dev was relieved when Dr Sharma told him that an anti-rabies injection would not be necessary. Dev's neighbour had once been bitten by a dog suspected of having rabies and the neighbour had to be given sixteen injections in the stomach.

"Doctor Sahib, it was a huge mistake on my part to think that such a beast could be tamed. I will be glad to see the back of him."

"Forgive me for asking, but tell me, as I do not understand, why did you get the animal in the first place?"

Dev looked down at his aching bandaged hand. "My wife used to have a pet monkey when she was a child. We thought it would be educational for Kiran."

Dr Sharma looked baffled. "But Sardarji, you obtained him from Sohan, the *bazigaar*, no? He was in all likelihood a wild monkey. Surely, your daughter would have appreciated some other means of learning?"

Dev shifted uncomfortably on his chair. Kiran looked at Doctor Sharma with newly acquired admiration. Here was an astute man.

"Hindsight is a great gift, Doctor Sahib. We live and learn."

The conversation had become awkward but was interrupted by the noise of the front gate banging open.

It was Shankar and Sohan, the *bazigaar*, carrying between them a very solid looking cage.

Sohan began apologising as soon as he saw Dev. "So sorry, Sardarji. Thousands of apologies. I was told he was a good monkey. But he is not. He bites the hand that feeds him. And us."

Kiran found this hilarious. She had to pinch herself to stop bursting into laughter.

Sohan was earnest. He kept apologising over and over.

Jassi could see that he was genuinely upset and tried to comfort him. "Sohan, it's okay. Who knew this monkey would be like this? It is not your fault."

"But Bibiji, look at what this demon has done to Sardarji's hand? What if he had attacked yourself or your daughter after he was let loose? I will teach him a lesson he will not forget."

"No, Sohan," Dev interrupted. "You must promise me you will not beat him. It is not his fault. Please ensure that he is taken back to the foothills and released."

Sohan clasped his hands together. "But Sardarji, such a wicked thing to do after all your kindness to him."

"No," replied Dev. "It was not kind doing this to him. We are at fault. He is entitled to be free like us."

Dr Sharma and Sohan gaped at him. It was true then what people said about this Sardarji – he was indeed a very odd fellow.

"My husband is right," said Jassi. "Please ensure he is set free, back where he came from."

Sohan wiggled his head from side to side. "As you wish. I will take him now and return him to the forest, Sardarji."

With Puran and Shankar's help, Sohan dismantled the pole and put Shero in the cage. The monkey did not resist, and when the door slammed shut he looked at them all with baleful eyes. Shankar and Sohan tied the cage onto the back of the rickshaw that was normally used to transport goods from the farm to the house. Dev, Jassi and Dr Sharma were busy chatting so only Kiran was watching Shero as he was wheeled out of the yard in the cage in the back of the rickshaw.

He looked back at her and stuck out his tongue. Then he turned around and wiggled his bottom at her.

Kiran stared in disbelief. This monkey was not that wild. He knew how to shock a girl.

As the rickshaw disappeared around the corner, his bared bottom was the last she saw of him.

THE LOST HONOUR OF
LATA SHARMA

I

Renu Sharma peered over the balcony. Her best friend, Jyoti, was describing the holiday that her parents had planned for the summer, but Renu was only half listening as her eyes scanned the verandah below for her older sister.

Then she saw her.

Lata was sitting on the steps of one of the classrooms. As she tilted her head to move a wisp of hair from her eyes, the sun caught her watch briefly. She was completely absorbed in the book that was perched on her knees.

Lata was oblivious to the girls running around her, their high-pitched cries piercing the summer air. It was lunchtime and hundreds of girls were milling around the school grounds, some playing games whilst others ate food from their tiffin boxes and chatted loudly.

Renu spied on her sister as she had done countless times before from this balcony. It saddened her to see Lata on her own and lost in her book. She knew her sister was one of the brightest girls in the school. She was always top of her class and her teachers praised her diligence daily. However, Renu wished that Lata would make more of an effort to make friends.

Lata appeared not to mind her isolation. In fact she guarded it fiercely. Renu had realised long ago that her sister thought she did not need friends. When Renu tried to talk to her about it, Lata smiled and told her that she did not miss having friends, as books were her favourite and most loyal companions. They would secure her future as a world-class doctor and never let her down. The girls around them lacked ambition, she said. They would all be married by the time they left college, but Lata and Renu were different. They would be successful career women before they were married.

Renu listened carefully to Lata's words. She loved her sister deeply and they were very close. Lata was four years older than she was and very protective towards her younger sister. The only thing apart from books that Lata cared about was Renu.

II

Mutual acquaintances had suggested the match. Sunita and Raj, Lata's parents, had been impressed by the information provided about their prospective son-in-law. His family was respectable and their enquiries had not disclosed any skeletons in the cupboard. Sanjay was a handsome, Indian-born, American-educated businessman who ran care homes for the elderly in California. He was an only son. His parents, Manoj and Gita, accompanied him when he came to Lata's house for the initial meeting.

Sunita and Raj greeted them at the front door. Sanjay was dressed smartly in a white open-neck shirt, navy blazer and sand-coloured chino trousers. When Raj took his hand, Sanjay reciprocated with a firm handshake. He gave them a warm smile then confidently strode into the house as though he were a regular visitor.

Lata had been told to wait in the kitchen until she was summoned. She felt very nervous and had been pacing restlessly when Keesho, the maid, opened the door and beckoned her to join the others. She moved forward to greet the guests with hands together in the traditional way, keeping her eyes lowered. She sat down next to her mother on the sofa, the sequins on her electric blue *sari* shimmering prettily.

Sanjay's parents chatted away. Manoj told them about Sanjay's business and house in California. Clearly, he was very proud of his son and his achievements. Sanjay glanced at Lata occasionally. He thought she looked attractive. She was a bit on the thin side, but all the girls he had been introduced to in India as possible matrimonial partners seemed to look like this. So far, none had taken his fancy. He was not looking for a demure wife; he wanted an equal. Somebody who would be comfortable with his western friends and lifestyle, share his ideas of fun and laughter and enjoy socialising.

Sanjay's mother, Gita, leaned forward and looked directly at Lata. "So *beti*," she said, "you're a doctor at the civil hospital at the moment, is that right?"

"Yes," Lata replied, keeping her eyes cast down. Gita smiled. The girl was shy, she thought, just as she was when first introduced to Manoj all those years ago.

"What area of medicine do you specialise in?" she said.

"Presently, general work in the accident and emergency ward," Lata replied. She felt acutely anxious at being in the spotlight and wished Gita would stop asking her questions. Then, as if the Gods were listening, Keesho entered the room with a tray of food and drinks. Sunita and Lata got up and helped place everything on the table before serving everybody.

Sanjay's parents chatted away as they ate the *samosas*, *pakoras* and other snacks. Sanjay watched Lata. Suddenly, she looked up and caught him staring. As their eyes met, she felt startled. She had seen the photos provided by Sanjay's family, but here in the flesh he looked so handsome. He had dark brown eyes with long lashes that made him look as if was wearing mascara. Now he was smiling at her. Suddenly he winked at her! Her eyes opened wide in astonished delight.

Gita had witnessed her son's mischief. She touched her husband's arm lightly and said, "Perhaps we ought to allow Sanjay and Lata some time for a chat so they can get to know each other better."

Raj and Sunita did not look surprised. The matchmaker had warned them this was a progressive family who might make such a suggestion. They had agreed to allow it. Things had changed in India, with couples now expecting a chance to chat before agreeing to a marriage. Gone were the days when the bride and groom did not meet until the wedding day.

"Of course," said Raj. "Perhaps Lata would like to show Sanjay the garden. It's Sunita's pride and joy."

Sanjay stood up quickly. "That would be great," he said. "Lead the way."

Lata blushed as she got up. She felt everyone's eyes upon her. If only Renu were here, she thought. But Renu was thousands of miles away in London, studying.

Lata walked nervously in front of Sanjay. As she opened the French doors overlooking the garden, she heard Sanjay whistle slowly.

"How beautiful! Clearly, your mother has green fingers."

"Yes," replied Lata, "my mother loves this garden and tends to it every day."

"It shows it is loved," said Sanjay, with a mischievous glint in his eyes. "So, tell me, Lataji, what are your interests? What do you do for fun?"

Lata did not know what to say. She had met a few suitors but this one struck her as particularly forward.

"I like doing lots of things," she stammered.

"Like what? More details, please," he insisted.

She bit her bottom lip, feeling embarrassed and wishing Renu were there.

"I like books. Reading. Keeping up with current affairs. That kind of thing."

He threw his head back and laughed.

"Well, that's all really good. But what do you do for fun?"

"I like watching films and helping my mother with the garden. But often I have to do long shifts at the hospital, so my personal time is limited."

He nodded as though he understood. She is very shy, he thought. This was not a problem. When they got to know each other better, it would be fine.

"How do you feel about living in America?" he asked.

For a moment she looked thoughtful. "Very excited," she said. "My younger sister, Renu, is studying in London but I have never travelled outside of India. Renu has also travelled to the States. She says it's amazing. So much to see and do."

He looked at her with a grin. She had suddenly become more animated. He was right, he thought, she already seemed less anxious and more comfortable.

"Would you be happy meeting up for lunch or dinner soon?" he asked. "So that we can get to know each other better? I don't want to feel as if I'm marrying a stranger." He laughed.

She thought for a moment. "I would, provided my parents have no objection."

"Of course," he replied. "I understand. It's India. I respect that and admire your directness. I think you and I are going to get on just fine."

III

The engagement party took place a fortnight later. In a few weeks Sanjay had to return to the States, and his parents wanted the wedding to take place before then. Renu could not attend as she was in the middle of her final exams, but she promised to be at the wedding. Lata was disappointed but knew how important it was for Renu to finish her degree. She consoled herself with the knowledge that Renu would be home in time for the wedding. She really wanted Sanjay to meet her.

Lata's parents had never witnessed their daughter so happy. Since her engagement to Sanjay, she radiated delight. The couple met regularly with the blessing of their parents and seemed constantly on the phone to each other. Sometimes they went to a cafe for coffee and cake, or to a restaurant or cinema. Lata had never before received such attention. Sanjay sent her flowers, messages and letters, and gave her extravagant gifts. He told her about his business in America, describing his lifestyle and house in California. He explained that he loved travelling and described the many places he had visited, the sights he had seen and the people he had met.

She was surprised when he told her about his friends. She did not expect so many to be women. Sanjay seemed relaxed about this and told her that when you live in America it was not unusual to have friends of both sexes. India was still living in the dark ages in his view which was why, he said, he could never live in India.

She became shy when he described his desire to have children. As an only child, Sanjay felt he had missed out. Though he had many cousins, he told her that he had always wanted a sister or a brother. He said he was pleased to be gaining a sister-in-law. He had not met Renu but he had spoken to her on the phone and Lata was clearly very fond of her younger sister. Whenever she talked about her, her eyes lit up and her voice could not disguise her pride.

Lata became infatuated. She could not wait to see Sanjay and thought of him constantly throughout the day. She could not believe her good fortune. She would have a westernised, liberal husband.

Lata had no male friends. In fact, she had no female friends either. Renu was her best friend and confidante. When Sanjay asked about her friends, she described her work colleagues because she did not want him thinking that she had none. But this did not work for long as Sanjay began commenting that he had never met them. He joked that her friends were avoiding him.

As time went on, Lata's letters and calls to Sanjay revealed the intensity of her feelings for him. She told him she would die if she could not see him every day. She became sullen and argumentative if other commitments made him miss a date. Sanjay began to feel stifled by her constant need to talk to him and be with him. At first he had been flattered, but as time went on he became concerned. After all, like him, she was an educated and modern person, unfettered by the conventions of their parents' generation. He pressed her about her friends and interests and eventually realised that she had none. Her work was her only focus. She could talk for hours about the A&E cases she was dealing with. It began to dawn on him that they had very little in common.

Sanjay was an extrovert and loved socialising. He was confident and spoke to everybody he met, appearing genuinely interested in them. Lata, on the other hand, was awkward and shy. She would gaze at him in wonder. When he introduced her to his friends and cousins, she would exchange greetings but seemed unable to hold a conversation.

Once, he had asked her how she would feel about going to work as a doctor in America when they moved there after the wedding. She replied that she could work in his care homes so they could be together during the day.

This troubled him. He wanted a wife who was independent, not one who needed to be with him twenty-four-seven. It took him a week to make the decision that he could not marry her. They were incompatible. She stifled him. He decided to let her down lightly but he felt very guilty. He would tell her that his businesses were failing and he was broke. She would understand, he thought. He also decided that his parents were wrong about him finding a wife in India. He would return to California and look there.

IV

It was her mother who found her. She had made some *masala* tea and called to Lata in her room but Lata had not answered.

"She will have her nose stuck in some medical book," thought Sunita as she poured the tea into a cup and carried it upstairs to Lata's room.

Raj and Sunita had been worried about their eldest daughter since Sanjay dropped his bombshell. He had done it over the phone, which seemed a cowardly way to break somebody's heart. At first, Lata had been mute with shock. Then came the tidal waves of tears and pleading. She promised to change in any way he wanted and begged him not to do this for the sake of her and her family's *izzat* or honour. But Sanjay's mind was made up. He said he was sorry and that, given time, she would find a suitable suitor. After he ended the call, Lata sat in stunned silence. She had not been herself since. She had stopped eating and washing and just sat around the house looking listless. She told the hospital she was unwell and would not be at work for a week or two.

The day her mother brought her tea, she had tied her scarf around her neck and tethered it to the ceiling fan. As a doctor, she knew how strangulation worked. She had treated many women who had tried to end their lives in this way: women whose in-laws said their dowries were insufficient, women who had only borne girl children or who had been beaten to a pulp by their husbands and could bear no more. She hoped it would not take too long.

Her mother opened the bedroom door to find her daughter dangling. The cup of tea fell from her hands. She shrieked as she rushed forward to hold up Lata's body.

"Help! Someone help!" she screamed. "Please! No! No! Lata! Oh Lata! No! No!"

Tears poured down her face as she bore her daughter's weight. She had once been such a tiny featherweight baby, her beautiful Lata.

Down in his office, Raj heard his wife scream. He sprinted up the stairs, ran into Lata's room and took the weight of Lata's body from his wife.

"Quick! Get me a knife or some scissors."

Sunita ran downstairs and grabbed a knife from the kitchen. She tripped and almost fell on the blade as she stumbled up the stairs to hand it to Raj. Hearing the commotion, Keesho and Sham, the driver, came running. Sham helped Raj whilst Keesho held Sunita, who was ashen-faced and looked like she was going to faint.

"Sham, hold her," said Raj as he leapt on a chair and began frantically tearing at Lata's *dupatta* with the knife. With a few hard strokes he cut her loose. He felt the weight of her body in his arms as she slid to the floor. Her eyes were shut and she appeared not to be breathing.

Sunita broke free of Keesho's embrace. She knelt beside Lata's body and began stroking her daughter's face, saying her name over and over. Raj knelt down beside them and gave Lata mouth-to-mouth resuscitation. He saw that she was breathing after all. He quickly picked her up and with Sham's help carried her downstairs to the car. They placed her limp body on the back seat. Sunita squeezed in and held Lata whilst Raj jumped in the front and yelled at Sham to drive to the hospital. The car screeched down the driveway and onto the main road.

V

With tears in her eyes, Renu stood on the verandah and watched her sister. Lata laughed as she played with Sham's two young children. Renu heard her talking to them in a baby voice.

What has happened to her? Renu thought. Her beautiful and intelligent sister had turned into a child. She could not bear the change. Whilst she knew that Lata had become infatuated with Sanjay, she could not comprehend why Lata would try to kill herself over him.

Renu felt so much anger towards Sanjay. What an arrogant, trumped up American-returned *desi*! He was a coward and a dishonourable man. It was the news that he had become engaged to a woman in California that had pushed Lata over the edge. Her family had tried to keep it from her, but she had overheard her father's angry phone conversation with his cousin in San Francisco. Raj was normally a calm man, but he had sworn during the call and threatened "to break that *harami*'s legs" if he ever crossed his path. Lata knew that the bastard in question was none other than Sanjay.

She had been depressed, tearful and withdrawn after Sanjay had broken off the engagement. How could he be so callous? Was he not ashamed of what he had done? Men from decent families did not go around making false promises to young women, breaking their hearts and ruining their lives.

Renu knew that Lata had been driven to this drastic action by the shame of rejection and the perceived stain on her family's honour. Because her parents had thought she was almost married to Sanjay, they had permitted her to be seen in public with him, holding his arm, giggling and spending hours alone with him. In the eyes of the community, her honour had been tarnished by a man who did not intend to marry her.

Hot tears ran down Renu's face as she recalled the frantic call her parents had made from the hospital. They did not know if Lata would live or die. While Lata lay in a coma Renu got a flight home to be at her sister's bedside.

When she eventually opened her eyes, Lata looked around the room with confusion. Her face did not register any recognition of her parents or Renu. The consultant had warned them there was a strong possibility that Lata would be brain damaged, as the *dupatta* had stopped the blood flow. Now she looked around with her innocent and child-like eyes, her brain devoid of intelligence. She might be a doctor but she would never again prescribe medication or treat anyone's symptoms.

Renu hoped that Lata would get better. She would ensure that her sister got the best care. As she gazed at her, she recalled how she used to watch her from the school balcony, worrying that she did not have any friends. She remembered her sister's determination to be an independent career woman. As tears filled her eyes, Renu longed more than anything in the world to have the old Lata back. But that Lata Sharma was never coming back. She had died the day her heart had been broken and her honour had been lost.

A MONUMENTAL LOVE

I

Nargis stared, her mouth half open in amazement. Although she had seen many photographs of the Taj Mahal before, nothing prepared her for the stunning vision before her. The sun reflected off the white marble, giving it a radiant glow. She remembered reading that it changed hue throughout the day as the sun rose and then set again, and she wanted to witness this.

She felt overwhelmed by the beauty of this monument to love and loss. She walked slowly towards it, careful not to bump into the crowds around her.

Built by the Mughal Emperor, Shah Jahan, in memory of his beloved wife Mumtaz Mahal, it took twenty-two years to complete. Thousands of workers from North India and beyond were involved in its creation and – this was her favourite fact – over one thousand elephants were used to transport materials.

Even her chatterbox husband, Richard, was left speechless. She felt his hand reach for hers as he walked alongside her towards the tomb's entrance. She squeezed his hand and they walked together as though in a trance.

II

Two months earlier in Birmingham, Nargis had retired from the general medical practice she had shared with Richard for over thirty years. They wanted to travel and spend more time with their children and grandchildren.

The practice was in a deprived part of Birmingham and they had worked hard to meet the demands of a growing patient list. Many were refugees and asylum seekers from Afghanistan, Pakistan and Somalia, and their English was limited.

Nargis and Richard Fisher were popular doctors.

Patients liked their courteous manner. There was much sadness in the community when they decided to retire, as empathetic doctors were hard to come by. Nargis spoke Urdu and Punjabi, which was a great bonus as far as many of her patients were concerned.

They had sold their practice and said their farewells. The sale had been lucrative, and now they were planning their travels. Nargis had insisted on visiting India and Richard had no problem agreeing. Although they had visited Nargis's family in Pakistan many times, she had always wanted to visit India. The Indian High Commission had granted them visas after much communication and several visits in person to the Commission office. Their three children, Rafiq, Sabrina and Amir, had helped them plan their itinerary and book their flights. They planned to visit New Delhi, Agra, Jaipur and Jalandhar during their trip.

They had arrived in New Delhi two days earlier. Nargis had insisted that they visit the Taj Mahal first and spend time exploring New Delhi on their return. She had been quite clear that Jalandhar should be their final destination. Richard went along with her plans. He loved his wife and knew how long she had waited to make this journey.

They had caught the train from New Delhi to Agra the day before and booked into a luxury hotel. Later, they would explore the Agra fort where Shah Jahan's son, Aurangzeb, had imprisoned him, able only to view the shrine to his beloved by peering through a tiny window. But for now it was the Taj Mahal that held Nargis and Richard's attention.

III

Jusapur, Punjab, India. November 1947

Karan Singh made his way from his fields to his home in Jusapur village. It had been a long day. First, he had to milk his two cows then drop off the milk to his neighbours' houses. Then he walked to the fields where he spent the day ploughing, digging and watering. He was tired, hungry, and dirty, and couldn't wait to get home.

As he approached the village, he saw two men grappling with a young woman. He did not recognise any of them. It was clear that the woman was distressed and as he got nearer he heard her shrieks of terror.

When she saw him, she called out, "Help me! Please help me!"

Karan Singh was an ex-teacher. He had taught

mathematics in a boys' school in Lahore for many years. It was a job that he loved and he was an excellent teacher. His patience and good humour had made him popular with his pupils and work colleagues alike. He shared a flat with a couple of the other teachers. The parents of his pupils appreciated the progress that their sons were making in maths, and this, combined with the fact that they knew he was a single man, meant that he had no shortage of invitations to come and share food and celebrate festivals. Given the mixed nature of the school, he had attended Muslim, Hindu and Sikh festivals during these years in Lahore.

Karan Singh had chosen not to marry because he had witnessed his father's anguish when his wife, Satnam Kaur, had suddenly died. His parents had been devoted to each other and Mota Singh, Karan Singh's father, had never recovered from the loss. Mota Singh had tried to encourage Karan Singh to marry, but he resisted and Mota Singh refused to pressurise his son despite comments from other family members.

When Mota Singh had fallen ill, he wrote to his only son asking him to come home to take over the running of the family farm. Without hesitation, Karan Singh handed in his resignation and returned to Jusapur where he threw himself into farming and looking after his ailing father. He missed his old school terribly but he never complained or let his father know how he felt. He knew that his father had made many sacrifices to enable him to get an education and pursue his love of teaching in a city that was miles away. Although Mota Singh was uneducated, he was a good and wise man who loved his son deeply. Karan Singh wept bitterly when his father passed away shortly after his return, but he vowed to carry on looking after the farm as he knew this was what his father had wanted.

When the partition of India was announced, Karan Singh realised that his beloved school in Lahore was going to be in the new West Pakistan. He grew anxious because he sensed a bloodbath would follow, and he was not wrong. Later, when he witnessed the treatment of the Muslim families fleeing from Jusapur, he was in despair at the fact he could do nothing to stop it. People who had grown up harmoniously together with their neighbours were butchering each other with a ferocity and hatred that previously would have been unimaginable.

He was relieved that his father had not lived to witness the violence. Many of the Muslims attacked and driven out of Jusapur had been his friends.

Mota Singh was an honourable man and had taught his son well. So when Karan Singh now saw two young thugs attacking a young woman before his very eyes, he knew he had to intervene.

"What's going on here?" he said.

"What's it to you, old man?" one of the men snarled.

Like Karan Singh, he was a bearded Sikh and he wore a blue turban and a white *kurta* pyjama.

The woman could not have been more than eighteen years old. She was slightly built, her brown eyes desperate with fear. There was a tear in the left leg of her *salwar* and her *kameez* was ripped at the neck.

Karan Singh guessed that she had been taken from a family fleeing the violence that was spreading across the Punjab since the declaration of Independence and the creation of the two new nations of India and Pakistan.

"Wait! Wait!" Karan Singh said. "I may be able to help. What are you doing with her?"

The men looked at each other and laughed.

"Why?" said the second man who was wearing a green turban and had the wispy beginnings of a beard on his chin and a scar under his right eye. "Want some, Uncle?" he laughed pointing at the woman, who began to wail.

Karan Singh glanced at the woman whose wails became louder. What Karan Singh said next was a surprise even to him.

"How much?"

"To you, *chacha*," said the second man, "two thousand rupees."

Karan Singh did not have that amount of money to hand. He knew that these men were not the kind to hang around while he found more.

"I'll give you one thousand rupees, right now. It's all I have."

The two men exchanged glances. "Eighteen hundred rupees," the first man said.

"One thousand rupees is all I have," Karan Singh replied, "but I can give you a gold ring too."

The men looked at each other and nodded.

"She's yours, old man. Where's the money?"

"She's not to be touched until I get back, otherwise the deal is off."

The men smirked. The second man said, "Too late, *chacha*. I think she's been touched already."

Karan Singh ran to his house. He quickly located the cash and ring and concealed his dagger under the waistband of his pyjamas. As he ran out the door, he grabbed his blanket off the back of a chair. The trio were waiting for him at the same spot.

The men grabbed the money and ring and counted the cash. Karan Singh touched the dagger under his shirt. He was ready for anything if things got ugly.

The men spat at the woman and pushed her towards him.

"Young meat for you old man, but not halal," said the first man and they roared with laughter as they ran off towards the fields.

Karan Singh took the blanket and put it over the young woman's shoulders. She was weeping and shaking.

"Don't cry," he said. "You're safe with me. Come."

He led her back to his house.

IV

Four months had passed since Karan Singh rescued Shanaz.

At first it had been difficult and she cried almost every day. But as time went on she realised that Karan Singh was a good man. He spoke to her respectfully and did not have any expectations of her. He bought her new clothes and shoes and in return she started to help him with the day-to-day work around the house and in the fields.

She reckoned he was about forty years old. He showed her photographs of himself at the school in Lahore. He often spoke about his ex-pupils and his fellow school teachers with whom he had lost contact, wondering where they were. When he spoke about the violence, he became upset. He could not believe that friends and neighbours could turn on each other the way they had.

On the day he bought her, she had been walking along the Grand Trunk Road with her family. Otherwise known as the GT Road, it snaked its way from Chittagong in East India to Kabul in Afghanistan. It was the main route for refugees heading to the newly created Pakistan, or those coming the opposite way to India. The family had few belongings with them as they had to escape quickly from their home when the mob set fire to adjoining buildings. They had lived in a predominantly Muslim area on the outskirts of the city where Shanaz's father had worked as a clerk, but it was no longer safe for him to go to work.

Her parents and siblings – two younger brothers and a sister – were weary after walking all night through the dark. There were two other families walking with them, all were unarmed except for a few sticks that the men carried.

The GT Road was an hour away from the village of Jusapur. The convoy was attacked at daybreak by a group of men carrying swords and knives. In the commotion, Shanaz saw her parents thrown to the ground, beaten and struck with swords. Her brothers were kicked, punched and stabbed, and she saw her younger sister dragged away by two men.

She too was grabbed and slapped. She felt hands on her body before she was hoisted onto somebody's shoulders. She struggled and bit into her abductor's shoulder only to receive a blow to her head in return. When she came to, she was lying in a field. She opened her eyes to see the two men who would later sell her to Karan Singh standing over her. They were rearranging their clothes.

This was as much as she was prepared to say. At this point, Karan Singh would also start weeping and they would hold each other until darkness fell.

V

It was her wedding day. Shanaz wore a red *salwar kameez*. Her hands and feet had been hennaed and on her wrists she wore red glass bangles, which tinkled when she moved.

Karan Singh beamed as he arrived on a white

horse, followed by a band of musicians playing enthusiastically and a small group of dancing relatives and villagers. He wore a starched red turban and a crisp white *kurta* pyjama, and embroidered Punjabi slippers with curled up toes. His beard had been oiled and he wore a sword across his body.

Shanaz recalled the day Karan Singh had asked her to marry him. He had been so nervous. He had returned from the city earlier in the day bringing her a box of her favourite sweets, *gulab jaman*.

She had said yes. His eyes glistened with tears as he held her hands in his own.

"You will never regret it. You have made me the happiest man on earth!"

A year later, they celebrated the birth of their daughter, Roshni, and Karan Singh thought he might burst with joy. He distributed sweets to all his neighbours and family in celebration.

His neighbours laughed and said, "Karan Singh has gone mad! What man distributes sweets on the birth of a daughter?"

But Karan Singh was not a man to care about his neighbours laughing at him. His life had been empty but now was full of happiness.

VI

Nargis and Richard visited all the main tourist sites in New Delhi including the Red Fort, the Jama Masjid and India Gate. They also visited Connaught Place where they shopped and bought Punjabi suits for their daughter and daughters-in-law.

Now they were seated in first class on the Shatabadi Express, the fast train from New Delhi to Jalandhar and Amritsar. The railway station had been a challenge, but they found their seats and paid a porter to haul their luggage on board.

Richard noticed that Nargis seemed both anxious and excited at the prospect of this journey. She had sat down the night before and studied the map, marking the route of the train.

The train passed through green fields of sugar cane, and yellow fields of mustard and maize. To Richard, the landscape looked no different to many he had seen in Pakistan, but Nargis had her eyes glued to the window.

It was late in the evening when the train pulled in at Jalandhar. Their youngest son, Amir, had organised a hotel and car for them and they had no difficulty spotting the huge sign with DR FISHER written on it in large letters. The driver was a smiling young man with spiked hair and starched white shirt and trousers. He introduced himself as Sunil whilst securing their luggage in the car boot. Richard noticed that Nargis grew quieter as the car made its way through the grimy streets of Jalandhar. He tried to engage her in conversation but she seemed withdrawn, so he too became silent.

VII

Nargis kept twisting her scarf as she sat in the hotel room sipping a cup of tea. Richard was swimming in the pool downstairs and she felt guilty about enjoying his absence. She needed the time to gather her thoughts. She had not anticipated how difficult this journey was going to be, and her stomach churned as she reflected on her past.

She remembered her eleventh birthday. As always, her parents had arranged a party to celebrate. The house was ablaze with lights and delicious food had been brought in. Lavish presents had been bestowed on her. Nargis was so happy. Her parents loved her so much.

It was her cousin, Jamila, who told her. She had never really liked Jamila, who was often spiteful to her. During the party, they were hiding together in the garden during a game of hide and seek. Jamila had looked at Nargis.

"You do know you're not really my cousin, don't you?"

"What do you mean?" Nargis replied.

"I mean we are not related. Uncle Javid and Auntie Farah adopted you when you were little."

Nargis could not speak. Her heart raced. She could hear her mother calling her but she couldn't answer. Jamila got up and ran inside the house.

Her mother searched the garden until she found Nargis sitting under a bush crying.

"What is it dearest?" her mother asked.

Nargis looked down at the ground.

"Jamila said you're not my mother!"

Her mother looked startled. She carefully moved the branches of the bush and sat down next to Nargis taking her in her arms.

"I may not have given birth to you, Nargis, but you are my child and I cannot live without you. I promise you your father and I will answer all your questions later," she said with tears in her eyes.

Afterwards when all the guests had gone, her mother kept her promise. Dr Khan and his wife sat their daughter down and explained how they came to adopt her when she was barely three years old.

They told Nargis how her parents had been separated. Her mother, Shanaz, had been abducted whilst her family were fleeing to Pakistan during the Partition. Her father, Karan Singh, had bought her from her abductors. Under an agreement made between Pakistan and India, abducted girls and women had to be returned to their families. Someone had tipped off the police and, in accordance with the law, the police had removed Shanaz and returned her to her father's family in Lahore.

Shanaz had not wanted to go, saying that she was happy with her husband and child in India, but her family insisted on her being returned to them. It had taken Karan Singh over a year to locate his wife in Lahore by which time her family had married her off to a distant cousin and she was expecting a child. Karan Singh launched a case in court but Shanaz did not attend and her family said she was pregnant and unwell. A few days later, Karan Singh heard that Shanaz had died in childbirth, as had her baby son.

The judge in the case was Dr Khan's friend, Judge Ramzan. He had overstepped his remit by allowing the case to be heard, but he had been touched by Karan Singh's plight and love for his wife. Afterwards Karan Singh thanked him for his kindness.

A few days later, a little girl was found outside the judge's house with an envelope pinned to her dress. Inside were a note and five thousand rupees.

"You seem like a decent and kind man," Karan Singh had written. "Please take care of my daughter and find her a good home. I am enclosing money for her upkeep."

Judge Ramzan searched for Karan Singh but he was never found. So the judge told his friend, Dr Khan, about the child, knowing that the doctor and his wife were unable to have children. Without any hesitation, Dr Khan agreed to take the child.

Farah Khan fell in love with Roshni from the moment her husband brought her home. Before Roshni's arrival she had been depressed, but now all that was behind her. They changed her name to Nargis, believing that a Muslim name would ensure that she would not face any awkward questions about her origins in the future. She was the best thing that had happened to them. They always planned to tell her the truth about her childhood but Jamila had made the day come sooner than they had wanted. As Nargis sat between them on the sofa listening to them, she saw the love in their eyes, and that made her love her parents more than ever.

VII

The car made its way along the congested GT Road towards Jusapur. Nargis had seen the surprise on the face of their driver, Sunil, when she told him their destination. He had been well trained and did not ask questions other than to check that she meant the Jusapur that was on the road to Amritsar. She could tell he was intrigued by the Punjabi-speaking Muslim woman with the white doctor husband. It made her smile. He probably assumed she was a housewife and the doctor referred to in the booking was her husband. And now, they wanted to visit a village rather than go to Chandigarh or Amritsar, where tourists normally asked to be taken.

Nargis looked out the window. She did not know what she was looking for, but she knew she had to make this journey. Richard looked across at her with concern. He reached across and held her hand. She turned and looked at him and smiled.

Suddenly, the car turned off the main road and they found themselves on a dusty side road, which was sealed but not well maintained. The car jolted occasionally, and Sunil looked back at them in the driver's mirror.

"Sorry, sir. Sorry, madam. The road is not good."

Richard replied, "Take your time, Sunil. We do not want to damage your car."

They continued until they found themselves approaching a village. Some of the buildings looked abandoned but there were some grand-looking new ones too. People peered into the car as it passed them. Children ran behind shouting and laughing.

Nargis leaned forward.

"Sunil," she said, "please stop when you get to the centre of the village."

"Yes, madam. Almost there."

Soon, he stopped the car and Nargis and Richard got out. A number of villagers stopped and stared at them. A young man approached and Nargis smiled at him.

"I wonder if you can help us. We are looking for Karan Singh's house."

The man looked puzzled.

"Karan Singh?" he replied. "Not sure. But come with me please. We can ask at the *Shanaz Durwaza* – Shanaz Gate."

Nargis looked startled.

"The *Shanaz Durwaza*?"

"Yes," the man said. "It is where the elders sit. They know everybody in the village."

He led the way down the lane. Richard and Nargis

followed, leaving Sunil with the car. They turned a corner and there in front of them stood an impressive structure made of bricks and concrete that was like a smaller version of India Gate. It had a carved roof with something written above the entrance. As they approached, they could see a group of older men sitting inside, chatting amongst themselves.

The men grew silent as they approached. The young man led Richard and Nargis forward. After exchanging greetings, he explained to the men that the visitors were looking for Karan Singh's house. The men eyed them with surprise.

"*Kaun* Karan Singh? Which Karan Singh?" one of the men asked.

Nargis looked at him and replied in Punjabi.

"Karan Singh who was married to Shanaz Begum. He was once a farmer from this village."

Another of the old men looked at Nargis closely.

"Yes *beti*, yes child, but why do you want to know?"

Nargis always knew that this moment would come. She suspected that this old man had known Karan Singh.

"Karan Singh was my father and Shanaz was my mother. And this is my husband, Richard," she answered.

The old man stood up and hugged them both.

"You are Karan Singh and Shanaz Begum's daughter and therefore are a daughter and son-in-law of this village," he said. "And Karan Singh was a relative of mine. I knew him. He was a good kind man."

To Nargis and Richard's surprise, he began crying. The other men got up and comforted him. He wiped his tears.

"Where are my manners? Our daughter and her husband have visited us after so many years. Come with me."

He led them through the archway to a house a few minutes away.

At the house, they received a warm welcome. The old man told them that his name was Shankar and he was the son of Karan Singh's cousin. He introduced them to his family, his wife, two sons, daughters-in-law and numerous grandchildren. Men, women and children hugged them and hot *samosas*, *pakoras* and tea were placed in front of them.

As they ate, Nargis told them that her father had left her in the care of Judge Ramzan and she had been adopted by Dr Khan and his wife, Farah. Judge Ramzan had tried to find Karan Singh but he had disappeared without trace. She told them about her meeting Richard at university and about their three children and grandchildren, and showed them photos on her phone.

After they had finished eating, Shankar went inside the house and returned with a faded black and white photograph of a handsome couple on their wedding day. The man was wearing a turban and *kurta* pyjama. His beard was neatly groomed and his moustache had been turned up at the sides. He was standing next to a young woman who had her head covered in an ornately embellished scarf. She wore an embroidered Punjabi suit. Happiness seemed to radiate from them both, and unusually for a formal photograph of that time they were both smiling directly at the camera.

"These are your parents, Karan Singh and Shanaz Begum. This was taken on their wedding day."

Nargis took the photograph from him and studied it intently. Tears fell from her eyes as she tried to speak.

"May I keep the photo?" she asked.

"Of course, you must keep it. Your father left it with my father. Before he left with you for Pakistan, he sold his fields to my father. Later he wrote from Lahore to tell us that Shanaz had died giving birth, and he asked my father to sell the house and use the money to build a *durwaza* in memory of your mother. He said that he wanted his daughter to have somewhere to visit if she ever came looking for her parents in the village. So my father sold the house and built the Shanaz Gate. We never heard from Karan Singh again, and no one knew what happened to him or his daughter afterwards, until now."

Shankar looked at Nargis and wiped his eyes.

"I remember your parents well. Your mother was very kind to us kids and made us all *biryani* and your father played games with us. I remember dancing at your parents' wedding!"

He got up and embraced her.

"I even remember playing with you. You were so pretty in your brightly coloured *salwar kameez*. Karan Singh used to carry you on his shoulders everywhere and you were always happy. Your name was Roshni then. I am so happy that you found us."

Nargis returned his embrace and wept against his *kurta* as Shankar put his hand on her head and blessed her.

GLOSSARY

Afghanis – monetary unit of Afghanistan

Badmaash – hoodlum

Bas – finish

Beti – daughter or young girl

Bewakoof – fool

Bhangra – folk dance of the Punjab

Bhenji – respectful term used when addressing an
older sister

Bibiji – respectful term for mistress of the house

Chacha – uncle, father's younger brother

Chal – go

Desi – colloquial term used by Indians/expats
to describe themselves or things associated
with India

Duffa ho – get lost

Dupatta – scarf worn by women

Gidda – folk dance of Punjabi women

Gora – white male

Gurdwara – Sikh temple

Jaldi – quick

Jeldara – wealthy titled landowner

Ji – respectful term used with names

Khatum – end

Kheyiji – please speak

Kismet – fate

Kurta – loose collarless shirt normally knee length

Maharani – Queen

Masala – spice

Namaste – greeting

Nanaji – maternal grandfather

Nawab – Muslim prince or nobleman

Paisa – monetary unit of currency in India

Pakoras – fried spicy fritters made from
gram flour

Panditji – respectful term for wise and learned
Hindu man

Pukka – pure

Samosas – vegetable or meat-filled triangular
pastries

Sardarji – respectful term for turban wearing
Sikh man

Sharaab – alcohol

Waheguru – Sikh term for God

ACKNOWLEDGEMENTS

This has got be the best part of writing a book. I get to acknowledge the people who helped me along the way. Thanks to all of you, in particular to; David Steele, for his valuable comments, edits and feedback on earlier drafts.

Liz Woodcraft, for her advice, experience of publishing, and for answering my many questions.

Karen Procter, Jill Day, Kate Drury, Jackie Mollison, Viv Hayes, Yasmin Rehman, and Jocelyn Watson for reading and listening to these stories and for being terrific friends.

The doctors, nurses and other staff at Kings College Hospital, London, who do an excellent job in difficult circumstances. Thank goodness for the NHS!

Motiaji, my English teacher at school in Jalandhar, India, who encouraged me as a mischievous and bored teenager to write stories and read them out aloud to my classmates.

Gita Sahgal, for coaxing me to put pen to paper, I doubt very much that this book would ever have been completed without her gentle prodding.

Lucy Llewelyn and her team at Head & Heart for their assistance and patience in guiding me through the different stages involved, from tidying up a manuscript to producing the final product.

Harbhajan Kaur, my mum, for passing on to me her gift for storytelling, and to my sisters, Parmjit and Abnash, for bequeathing me a wealth of experiences from which to draw inspiration.

Finally, Paulette Keating, I could not have done this without you. Thank you.

About The Author

Ranjit Kaur was born in the United Kingdom. Her parents emigrated from the Punjab, India, in the mid-1950s to the Midlands.

In 1971, partly as a result of an increase in racist attacks, her family returned to India where she spent her teenage years. She later settled in Scotland with her mother and siblings.

She is a long-time campaigner for women's rights and the rights of minority groups and she worked for several years as the director of a legal charity. This is her first work of fiction and she now lives in London.

You can contact her at:
twitter: **@dancingmaharani**
facebook: **@dancingmaharani**

Printed in Great Britain
by Amazon